Wildflowers
FOR Anna Lee

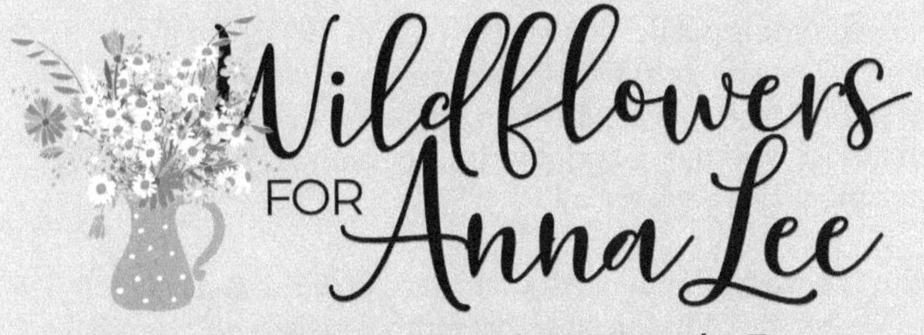 Wildflowers for Anna Lee

In Bloom Series Book 5

KASEY KENNEDY

Wildflowers for Anna Lee
In Bloom Series, Book 5

ISBN-13: 978-1-958942-13-0 (paperback)
ISBN-13: 978-1-958942-14-7 (hardcover)
ISBN-13: 978-1-958942-03-1 (e-book)

Cover design and interior formatting by Alt 19 Creative

Author Website:
www.kasey-kennedy.com

Published by:

To my grandma, Lula Troxell Walters Smith,
One of the greatest storytellers I've ever known.

"Love is like wildflowers; it's often found
in the most unlikely places."

– Ralph Waldo Emerson

AUTHOR'S NOTE

ORIGINALLY, I DID not intend for "Wildflowers for Anna Lee" to become a full novel. It was the prequel, a way to introduce the characters and the In Bloom world. In that prequel, Anna Lee met John Peerson at the steampunk festival, and they began to date. The prequel did not delve into all the challenges and emotions surrounding these two people meeting and falling in love.

As I worked on the series, John appears briefly in "Dahlias for Dominica", "Lilies for Lauren", and "Tulips for Tilly." He's mentioned as Anna Lee's beau, not much more.

In late 2023, I begin thinking about expanding the prequel into a full-length novel. I wanted more of Anna Lee's love story! As I began to think about that story and the timelines, I decided to make "Wildflowers for Anna Lee" book five in the series, instead of an extended prequel.

That raised a few issues with timelines. Being book five, logically its timeline should be after book four. But, since John is mentioned in earlier books, it overlaps with the timelines of previous books. So, in a way, we're going back in time in this story.

If you haven't read the previous books, then ignore everything I just said, and read on. Please enjoy "Wildflowers for Anna Lee"!

CHAPTER ONE

ANNA LEE FOSTER surveyed the retail space of In Bloom, her flower shop in Bloomington, IL. The grab-n-go bouquets were replenished, the counters were dusted, and her cat, Salty, who traveled back and forth to work with her, was sound asleep in the front window.

Unable to sit still, she moved about the store, straightening merchandise and checking her slim watch with the worn, leather band. It was a little before noon.

She would close the store soon and drive her scooter home to drop off Salty before begrudgingly riding back to the store to get the work van. She had a late lunch date with her cousin Tabitha, and they were meeting in Morton, a twenty-minute drive on the interstate, not a safe scooter ride for anyone, let alone a seventy-year-old.

Morton was a good meeting point for them, halfway between Bloomington and Peoria, where Tabitha lived.

"Anna Lee!" Tilly called.

Anna Lee strolled to the workroom doorway. "Yeah?"

"Do you want to look over this order to make sure they sent what you wanted before I put everything away?" Tilly stood by the long worktable with several open boxes in front of her.

"Naw. I'm sure you'll do fine, validating it. As long as you verify the counts against the invoice and make sure nothing is damaged, it'll be all right. If you see something strange, let me know."

"Sounds good!" The cheerful young lady smiled and got to work unpacking the boxes and putting the goods away. Her brunette ponytail swung back and forth, her professionally applied honey-colored highlights practically glowing.

Anna Lee loved being around the young ladies that worked for her. She loved their energy, their enthusiasm, and their zest for life. She liked to pretend they were her granddaughters; they were about the right age for that. When they came to her for advice, whether about boys, or friendships, or even schoolwork, she ensured that her advice was helpful. Words were important, and she wanted to provide nurturing words of wisdom. Words that would build someone up, not bring them down.

Words were powerful. Like wedding vows, they meant something. And like poisoned darts, they could pierce the skin and leave lasting wounds.

Anna Lee believed you could never apologize for something you said. If you said it, a part of you meant it. You couldn't "take back" your words. So, she made sure that she paid attention to the words that came out of her mouth.

Another important factor in hiring college students. They could put away supplies more easily than she. Anna Lee watched Tilly kneel to put things away on low shelves and stand up on her tippytoes to reach the tall shelves. She appreciated handing off the more physical aspects of running the flower shop to the girls. When she first opened the shop many, many years ago, she had no problem with all the physical chores, but now she didn't have the strength for it.

Twenty minutes later, Anna Lee was sitting on the stool behind the register, looking through a new seed catalog, when Tilly popped into the retail space.

"All right, all done," Tilly said, throwing her hands up into the air. The sleeves of her loose blouse swayed softly. "I think that does it for me. Are you sure there's nothing else I can help you with?"

Anna Lee shook her head before Tilly had finished her question. "No. I appreciate you putting that stuff away for me. Go on home. I'll close up soon and head out to have lunch with my cousin. Everything's stocked and ready for next week."

Tilly beamed. "Great! I'm going to see my roommate's new play tonight. She's immensely pumped. It should be great."

"Tell me all about it next week." Anna Lee brushed her gray bangs out of her eyes; she needed a bobby pin to keep her dry, wispy locks in place.

"Will do!" Tilly practically danced back out the door.

Oh, to have all that youth, beauty, and stamina. Wears me out just watching those kids.

ANNA LEE WALKED into Gloria's Diner and glanced around. She'd seen Tabitha's Impala in the parking lot, so she knew her cousin was here.

Tabitha's waving arm caught her attention, and she made her way over.

"I hope a booth is OK," Tabitha said as Anna Lee slid in opposite her.

"Don't mind me as I grunt and groan my way across." Anna Lee sat and shifted. "A chair's a little easier to get on and off, if you ask me."

"Noted, old lady."

Anna Lee only had five years on her cousin, so she took no offense.

"I'm thrilled you agreed to meet me. It's been forever since we got together," Tabitha continued, looking down at her menu.

"Yes. I wish you'd get to Bloomington more often." Anna Lee hated driving the van. "How are the boys?"

"Fine. Not much new there."

Tabitha's "boys" were in their thirties.

Anna Lee scanned the menu and decided on a bowl of chicken noodle soup. She hoped it was as good as hers.

Once the server took their orders, they got to the good stuff.

"You'll never guess my latest news." Tabitha smiled, her eyes twinkling behind her bright red eyeglass frames.

"Yeah?"

"My neighbor asked me out."

"Really? Are you ready to date again?"

Tabitha's husband, Frank, had died three years earlier, and up to this point, Tabitha had been adamant that she would never date again.

"Well, probably not." Tabitha looked down at the wedding band she'd moved to her right hand. "But I won't know until I try it. A little voice tells me Frank would be all right with it. I think the boys will be, too."

"Then you should give it a go." Anna Lee knocked on the table for emphasis. "But how well do you know this neighbor?"

Anna Lee had been looking out for her younger cousin's safety for over sixty years; she wasn't going to stop now.

"I know him very well." Tabitha took a sip of lemon-lime soda. "We've been neighbors for over ten years. He lost his wife last year."

"Didn't take him long to get back up on the horse. Make sure he's not dating you just to get you to do his cooking and cleaning."

"Hmm. Good point." Taking the focus off herself, Tabitha asked, "What about you? Any potential suitors?"

Anna Lee rolled her eyes. "At my age? Men come with either a divorce, a death, or dogs. No, thank you."

"Your age? You're only five years older than I am! There could be single men out there who aren't widowers or divorced or dog owners…" Tabitha's voice trailed off, like she knew the likelihood was slim to none. "A man doesn't have to take away from your life experience. One could add to it."

The server put their orders in front of them, and Anna Lee was glad for the distraction. She almost regretted meeting her cousin for lunch. She didn't want the pressure to date. Her life was full enough between her flower shop and taking care of her home and yard.

Changing the subject, Anna Lee turned the conversation back to Sam and Vic, Tabitha's sons. Those troublemakers were always worth catching up on.

HOME AFTER LUNCH with Tabitha, Anna Lee parked the van in her driveway and took her time going inside. She looked over the flower beds in the yard and glanced at the buds on the trees. Everything was waking from its winter's nap.

Thinking about naps, Anna Lee yawned and looked at her watch. It was only three. She could take a nap. Work, lunch and the hour driving to and from Morton had worn her out. A nap probably wouldn't disrupt her sleep tonight if she got one in soon.

As she entered her back door, Salty jumped off the dinette tabletop where he'd been staring out the window at the bird feeder.

"Oh, silly cat. You know you don't belong on that table," Anna Lee said, setting her pocketbook down. "I should move that feeder to the front yard. I don't mind when you sit on the back of the loveseat and look out the picture window."

She dropped some food in Salty's dish, and the cat quickly forgot his scolding. Putting a kettle on the stove for tea, Anna Lee sat at the dinette and grabbed her journal.

March 31st–Time to flip the calendar. Tomorrow is April Fool's. Wish I had someone to fool. When I was a kid, my parents and I played wonderful tricks on each other. Those were happy times. Before I became a teenager and messed everything up.

Met Tabitha for lunch and that woman's got a date. A date! My lord. She's sixty-five, what's she need a date for? She doesn't need financial help. Maybe she's bored. I wish her boys would settle down and give her some grandkids. Then she wouldn't be worried about that dating nonsense.

In the restaurant's parking lot, I discovered a small patch of wildflowers, and I picked a lovely bunch of blue phlox. When I got home, I put them in a blue mason jar. They look lovely sitting on the windowsill above the sink. Yes, I work with beautiful formal flowers–roses, irises, tulips, etc–on a daily basis, but wildflowers are my favorite. They have to work hard to make it. No one is coddling and tending to them. They just sprout and grow all on their lonesome, like me!

Driving home, I thought about my dates over the years. I could count on one hand the number of men I went out with after Gene died. So few, yet I still can't even remember all their names. Don't matter. They weren't special. Gene was. Maybe no one could live up to his memory.

I wonder what it would be like to date someone now. Would we have anything in common to talk about? All I know is flowers and gardening. And a little bit about repurposing stuff. That may be a lost art. We are living in such throwaway times. I hope the young people wake up and demand action for the environment. If we wear out this world, where are we going to live?

What really burns my bacon is all the climate deniers. Yelling so loudly that we must be wrong for worrying about it. But the oceans are heating up, the bugs, birds, and bees are dying. I can see that with my own eyes. Fewer of all of them since I was a kid. But yet, let's build more houses and freeways. And use more pesticides and chemicals in our food. That's a great idea.

Whew, I'm tired. I'd better get off my soapbox before I work myself up into a tizzy. Already feel my blood pressure boiling.

Maybe if I retired, I could get involved more to raise awareness, protest, write letters to officials, and advocate on behalf of the planet. "Anna Lee for Climate Action" would be my battle cry!

Now for that nap…

CHAPTER TWO

JOHN PEERSON CLOSED the door to his wife's closet. He'd thought today was the day he'd finally be able to pull the clothes out and ready them for donation. She'd been gone for five years. It seemed like it was finally time to let her belongings go.

But when he'd opened the closet, he could still smell a lingering whiff of her favorite perfume. And before he could pull one shirt or one dress off its hanger, he shut the door and walked away.

"There's no need to rush," he told himself. Though the clothes were showing heavy indentations where they rested on the hangers, and he worried they would be out of date before he could get them to a charity that could use them. People who needed the clothes probably weren't too concerned about whether the styles were current, he justified to himself as he let them hang, unused, a little longer.

Making his way into the kitchen, he refilled his coffee cup and sat at the table. He opened the Sunday paper and scanned the headlines. Nothing grabbed his attention. He'd found that more and more lately. Nothing held his interest for long unless it was a phone conversation or a visit from one of his daughters.

He checked the time, wanting to call his eldest, Kelley, before her day became busy caring for her young children. He knew

Sundays were their 'calm before the storm' day, as Kelley liked to call it. Their day to reset and ready themselves for the upcoming work week and daycare.

It was eight-thirty, and John decided it was as good a time as any to call her, so he picked up his phone and dialed her number.

"Hi, Dad!" Kelley said, answering on the first ring.

"Hello, Kells. How are you doing this morning?"

"Fine. Kids are still asleep. I'm letting them sleep in. Alex ran to the grocery store. If all goes well, I won't need to leave the house today. Though it's nice out, and it would be good to take the kiddos to the park. Let them run off some of their energy. What's your plan for today?"

John winced. He hated this question. Since his wife had died, he found his evenings and weekends at home filled with nothing that interested him. He roamed around his large home and tried to think of things to do. He'd move a lamp from one room to another, or wash the sheets on the guest beds, hoping for a guest, or he'd reorganize the bookcases. Nothing productive. He needed to get out more. He knew part of his lack of interest was depression, and he knew he should talk to his doctor about it.

Maybe he needed to bring more work home with him on the weekend. Why stop working on Friday at five?

"Well," he began. "I was thinking about taking the car to be washed and filling it up. Then I need to go to the store, pick up a few things. That's about it."

"Oh, Dad. Why don't you call Tara and ask her to dinner or something?"

Tara was his youngest, and at twenty-seven, she was busy with her own life.

"I might do that. Haven't talked to her since last weekend."

"Then it's time to call her. Speaking of eating, are you eating well?"

Kelley always worried about her dad, and John knew he needed to act more like the grown-up here. "I'm eating fine. Three squares a day and a snack. Or two," he added with a chuckle.

"That's good. I wish you'd try to date someone, Dad. Mom would want you to be happy. Not to be sitting around moping all day."

John bristled. "Who says I'm moping?"

"Are you?"

"No. I stay busy." He thought about the leak in the guest bathroom sink. He needed to fix that. "I don't think I'm moping."

"Fine. But it's still OK to date. We wish you would. I think you'd be happier if you found the right person to spend time with."

"When you say 'we' do you mean your sisters, or you and Alex?"

She hesitated. "Alex and I have talked about it. Deana and Tara might be a little slow to come around to the idea."

"I knew it. If they're not ready, then I'm not ready."

"Don't let them be your reason not to go out. They'll come around, Dad. I know it. I'll kick their butts if they don't. Oh… hold on."

John could tell Kelley had put the phone on mute. He imagined one of her kids waking up. Or maybe Alex had arrived home.

"Dad?" Kelley came back on the line. "Sorry, I gotta go. Joshua woke up and says he doesn't feel good. Call me later this week, OK? I love you."

"Love you. I will."

He hung up the phone and glanced around the kitchen. Why did talking to his girls make him happy and lonely at the same time? While he was on the phone with them, he was as happy as could be, but as soon as he hung up, the loneliness crept back in, and his bones ached.

He didn't need to wash the car; he'd done that yesterday. Looking in the refrigerator, he supposed he could get a half gallon of milk. Then going to the store wouldn't have to be a lie.

He closed the door and looked at the note behind the pink daisy magnet Deana had made in school. The to-do note said to call the doctor. He took it down and added, "call Tara".

CHAPTER THREE

ANNA LEE TIED her gardening apron around her waist and pulled on a pair of gloves. She picked up a pair of snips from the bench in her tool shed and made her way out the door. It was a glorious spring day, and she had a lot of yard work to do. It was Monday, her day off and she was going to take advantage of no rain and plentiful sunshine.

Salty darted under the row of peony bushes and Anna Lee wondered if the cat was chasing a mouse. If he was, she hoped he wouldn't bring it to her as a gift. Thanks, but no thanks.

She made her way to the far side of her yard and began pruning back a butterfly bush near the fence line, snipping the old branches and tossing them into the yard. She'd rake it later.

The robins were busy looking for worms, and songbirds were chirping overhead. Anna Lee felt like she had a piece of her own little heaven on earth. There was nothing better than being in her yard, watching the spring flowers bloom, trimming plants to help them grow, and listening to the birds as they sang their songs, as joyful as the day was long. Anna Lee whistled along with the birds. She might not be in tune with them, but she matched their delight.

The sound of a door slamming roused her from her interior monologue about the day, the outdoors, and the workweek ahead. Anna Lee glanced over to the neighbor's yard and watched as

Mrs. Samze approached. Her black and gray hair was worn up in a twist, and she wore a beige pantsuit with a latte-colored blouse. The woman always dressed nicely when she left the house.

"Good morning, Anna Lee!" her neighbor yelled.

"Mornin', Luellyn. How're you?"

"Finer than frog's hair. I see you're up and at it early today."

"Best time to be up and at it, I find."

"Right. Right. I'm heading to the store. Need anything?"

Anna Lee noticed the brown pocketbook and car keys in her neighbor's hand.

"Naw…well, wait. I could use some brown sugar. I want to bake some cookies this evening."

"No problem. I got you." Luellyn walked away, and Anna Lee lifted a hand in a half-hearted wave. She'd have to throw a few dollars in her pocket before Luellyn returned, so she could pay her for the sugar.

Anna Lee appreciated neighbors like that. Ones that looked out for you, didn't play the stereo too loudly, and kept a tidy yard.

Luellyn had been her neighbor for fifteen years. It was comforting knowing the woman was next door. Anna Lee assumed that if something happened to her, it wouldn't take Luellyn too long to come knocking and call the police if she didn't see the lights turning on or off or see Anna Lee coming and going.

You worried about those things when you lived alone. Anna Lee was fearful that she'd take a spill down the stairs or have a medical emergency and lie on the floor for hours or days before anyone noticed. She imagined Salty circling her, meowing in distress and unable to help. She made sure the bag of cat food was accessible to Salty. When his bowl was filled regularly, he'd leave it alone, but if something happened to her and the cat got desperate, she figured he could rip into the bag and help himself. That's why she also made sure the toilet bowl lids were up—so the cat would have access to water.

Working in the yard brought back memories of following her mother and grandmother around their yards. They'd taught her how to identify plants, how to prune them, how to take care of them, and which were friend or foe. She valued the old ways and folklore that her mother and grandmother had passed down to her. She just wished she herself had someone to pass the knowledge on to. Maybe she should write a book.

Having completed the pruning, she wiped her brow and tightened the scarf she had tied around her head to protect her ears from the wind. She proceeded down the row of plants and stood to admire the bleeding hearts that had recently bloomed. She loved the fun shape and colors of the red, pink, and white varieties in her yard.

They were an unusual plant in that they made her smile, but they also pulled at her heartstrings. She never understood why. Maybe it was the legends and folklore about bleeding hearts that made them rueful gifts in the garden. The Greeks said that they came from Venus' tears as she mourned the loss of her true love, Adonis.

Bleeding hearts always made her think about Gene. When he died, her heart had bled for him, and each time she looked at them, she felt a brief longing in her heart. She had once considered digging them up and tossing them, but decided their beauty was worth the sadness.

"A lonely flower for a lonely old woman," she muttered to herself as she lifted a small branch loaded with blooms. She let them go and turned around.

"Salty," she called, wondering where the feline was. "It's time for a treat. Let's go in and sit a spell."

Her large orange tabby cat came quickly; he loved the word "treat". She trudged up the back porch steps and opened the door to her three-story, pink Victorian home. Its purple and white trim may have been over the top to some people, but Anna Lee felt it suited her perfectly. Colorful, decorative, aging, with a few nicks and scrapes here and there.

SHE DROPPED A few treats into Salty's dish and made a piece of toast for herself. After filling her coffee cup and adding a splash of milk, she headed to the table and grabbed her journal. Before opening it, she picked up her wallet and pulled three dollar bills out of it. *That should be enough for the brown sugar,* she thought. She folded the bills and put them in the pocket of her apron, since the pants she was wearing didn't have any pockets.

Monday, April 2nd–Any day filled with work in the yard is a great day, and today was almost perfect.

Got to fill my lungs with fresh air, dig into the dirt, and walk around barefoot, soaking up the earth's goodness. Renewed my wild-woman energy. Talked to nature, talked to my ancestors, and talked to myself.

The bleeding hearts are blooming. Beautiful little blooms. Every time they begin to bloom, I relive the loss of Gene again. When his sister called me to tell me, I fainted right there in the kitchen, in front of my mom. I had just figured out I was pregnant. Knowing that he would not come home to help me take care of our baby was devastating. Another tragic story from that damn war.

On a happier note, Luellyn went to the store, and I asked her for brown sugar so I can make chocolate chip and pecan cookies. I'll mix up a full batch, but only bake a few and put the rest of the batter in the freezer. Good to have some on hand. Just in case unexpected company drops by.

Still thinking about lunch with Tab on Sat. Can't believe she's going on a date. Well, I can't blame her for wanting company. There are times I wish I had a companion. Someone to talk to. Someone who can talk back, unlike Salty. I amble around this big old house, and I see bedrooms that haven't had an overnight guest in twenty years. There was a time when Tabby and her boys would come and stay with me. We'd have a lovely time, trying to teach the boys pinochle and other card games. They'd bore quickly. Cards never had bells and whistles like their video games.

Maybe someday one of the boys will marry and have kids and they could come and stay. Though with their current trajectory, that won't happen in my lifetime.

Maybe I should think about selling this place and finding something smaller. But I would hate leaving my beautiful yard and all the flowers I've nurtured over the years. My peony trees, my asters, tulips…I could go on and on.

Tabby and I could get a place together. Now that her boys are grown, her house is too big for her, too.

But I'm not moving to Peoria. She could move here. Or we could pack up and move south. I've heard good things about Tennessee. Or maybe one of the Carolinas. And the winters wouldn't be so cold. Sometimes I think my fingers will freeze and fall off when it gets so cold.

Though moving out of state may make it harder for my daughter to find me if she ever tries to. Don't know if she knows she was adopted. Maybe she doesn't even know I exist. Maybe I could look for her. Naw, I'd be too afraid she'd reject me. Best just to imagine she's had a good, happy life. That's what I wanted for her when I let her go.

Now, everything hurts—my head, my body, and my heart. Knew I shouldn't have sat down.

September 27, 1991–Closed on the house today! I have a hand cramp after signing so many papers. My first house and who knows, it may be my only house.

It took my breath away the first time I saw it. Now, it's run down and needs a ton of work, but I'm ready to go. I can restore it to its former glory.

It's a mess, to be honest. The exterior walls are an ugly, ugly! lime green and the trim is a lemon yellow. Yuck! Must have been a good paint sale. But it's all chipped and peeling. Walking around outside, you can see little flakes of paint everywhere. Oh well, gonna be a lot more chips before it's done. I'll have to scrape all three stories off before I can repaint. I'm thinking pink and purple. My favorite colors.

Weeds and ugly evergreen shrubs have taken over the yard. Those got to go, and soon. You can barely walk around without getting a bramble caught on your clothes.

There's a small garage which I'll use to house all my gardening supplies and my scooter. It's too small for a car and I never wanted a big gas-guzzler, anyway.

I sketched out some ideas on what to plant in the yard. I want it to be full of old-fashioned blooms. Hydrangeas, peonies, hostas, hollyhocks, and columbines. I want <u>ALL</u>

the flowers, really. Maybe some I could even grow for In Bloom, be my own supplier.

If all goes well, by my estimate, it may take me eight years to rehab it top to bottom. Or rather, bottom up, not counting the basement. I'm going to start in the heart of the home, the kitchen. The kitchen is on the main floor. This house was subdivided into apartments over the years, so there are technically two kitchenettes on the second floor and one on the third. I'll tear all of them out. This will be a single-family home again while I'm here.

The first floor will have the sunny kitchen, overlooking the screened-in back porch and yard, a large dining room, with two corner mahogany built-ins (thank goodness no one ripped those out), a small back den, a formal living room, and a woman's parlor.

The second floor will eventually have four bedrooms and a shared hall bath.

The third floor will be a large, open space with light. It will be my craft and hobby room. That way all my in-progress projects will be out of sight of company.

Can't wait to have the first sleep-over with Tabitha and her family. The little boys will have a ball, running back and forth in the attic, when they get older.

Did I mention the turret? I envision building a curved bench window seat on both the second and third floors, so I can sit and look out at the view. The first-floor area is part of the women's parlor. I'll put two wingback chairs there with a small tea table in front of them, for entertaining.

Yes, it's probably more room than a single woman needs, but I want to restore it to its original purpose — a home for a large family. Unless I marry a man with half a dozen kids, it won't have a large family in my lifetime. I'm 39 now, the only way I'm having a family is if I marry into one.

Or, of course, if my daughter ever tries to find me. She's an adult now, 22. If she knows she was adopted, she could search me out. I still hold onto that dream. I always will. Maybe someday she'll get to see this house. It's my greatest wish.

CHAPTER FOUR

JOHN MET HIS daughter Tara for dinner on Wednesday at a new gastropub near the college. He'd prefer steak, but Tara wanted to try this place out. "Everyone is raving about it, Dad," she'd said, and he wanted to please his youngest.

After the server brought their drinks, an apple martini for her and a decaf coffee for him, John asked about her job and listened intently to the challenges she was facing.

She sat up straighter and leaned forward. "Things are good…" She drew out the word. "But not great. I just had my review, and my boss wants me to take on some additional responsibilities. To show my leadership abilities, he says. I thought I was doing that already. I don't know why he doesn't see it."

"Oh." John paused, nodding his head. He chose his words carefully so Tara wouldn't get defensive. "I see. Did you ask clarifying questions to get more details about what he was expecting?"

"No," she huffed. "I didn't want to look stupid. I just said OK. Now I'm in a pickle."

"That would be a pickle. My advice would be to prepare for your next meeting with him. Create a list of the things you are doing to show leadership, and then ask him what else he has in mind. Don't be defensive—"

"I'm not!"

John raised an eyebrow at her. She sat back in her chair and mouthed "sorry." He continued, "Don't be defensive, and ask him to clarify his response if you need him to. Don't walk out of there unclear on his expectations."

"Fine." She picked up her martini glass and took a long sip. Good thing she'd walked from her apartment and could walk home.

John marveled at how he could see both a twenty-seven-year-old woman and a seven-year-old child before him at the same time. He was sure he'd had the same conversation with her twenty years ago, when a boy teased her in class.

"Are you seeing anyone?" he asked, after they had exhausted the conversation about work.

"Nothing serious. A few dates here and there." She was being vague, and it bothered him. How would he know if he needed to intervene if she was being bullied or abused? He didn't expect every detail of his daughter's dating life, but he didn't like feeling as though he was being shut out.

"You will tell me if something gets serious, won't you?" he teased.

"Yes, Dad." She tilted her head and her short blond hair hit her shoulder. "But I'm not in any hurry to settle down. My career comes first."

He fiddled with his coffee cup and wished their dinners would arrive soon. He was hungry. "I understand that, and I want you to be happy. If you never marry, I'll be fine as long as you're happy."

He thought of his own situation. After his wife had died, he thought he'd be fine being single for the rest of his life. But now he wondered if maybe there would be a benefit in meeting someone, and maybe, just maybe, finding someone he could love for the rest of his days.

"I'm happy," Tara insisted. "I'll tell you if I'm not."

The server arrived and interrupted the conversation. John looked around the restaurant. All the other patrons appeared to be college students or young professionals like Tara. Where would someone in his late sixties even look for a romantic interest? There was no way he was using an app for that. He refused to use an app for banking. No way was he using one to find a date.

Maybe he needed to join a club or volunteer. Someone had said there was a program at the local community college about finding volunteer opportunities. They said there was even an app to find things you might be interested in. Now that he would use an app for.

Once the server walked away, Tara leaned forward. "What about you, Dad? Are you happy?"

John thought about the upcoming appointment with his doctor when he would mention his lack of interest and feelings of sadness. He might be depressed, but he'd never say that to his daughter.

"I'm fine. I'm looking into volunteering, to stay busy on the weekends and evenings if I can." Shoot. He'd have to follow through on that now.

"That's great!" Tara took a bite of the minuscule piece of chicken on her plate. He thought she might have two more bites left. "But you don't think it's too much? Don't you still work a ton of hours?"

"No, I stay close to forty now." His boss wouldn't let him work more than that. "Volunteering might fill some of the void. I hope I can find volunteer work that would be a good fit for me. Maybe meet some new people. You know. I was talking to Kelley over the weekend, and she was encouraging me to get out there and date."

He watched closely for Tara's reaction. Whenever this subject had come up in the past, she'd usually resorted to tears. It was probably smart to have brought it up here, in public, the coward's way.

Tara took a sharp breath. "She did, huh?" She chewed, contemplating. "Are you sure you're ready for that, Daddy? I mean, it's only been a few years since Mom…"

"Five." He kept his voice steady and calm. "It's been five years, Tara."

"You don't have to remind me," she snapped. "I count it out every morning when I wake up and remember she's not here." Her words were clipped, and he noticed she was blinking rapidly.

"The public" would not keep those tears from falling, he realized.

He reached over and placed a hand on hers. "I'm sorry. I didn't mean to upset you."

She sighed and leaned back, tilting her head back and blinking rapidly. "I should have worn waterproof mascara."

Bringing her gaze back to him, she frowned, and he wanted to rewind the last two minutes of the conversation.

Finally, she spoke. "If you want to date, that's fine. I'm sure Mom would be thrilled." She looked down and stabbed another piece of chicken.

John sucked in a breath. That hurt. Why did he think he needed her permission to date, anyway? He didn't, but he'd hoped she would be happy for him. Maybe it was too much to ask of his youngest daughter, who had adored her mother.

Changing the subject, he asked her if he could look for a baseball game for them to attend together that summer. Not having any sons, he was thankful that his youngest had become a baseball fan like her old man.

"Sure." She nodded, seemingly thankful for the change in topic. "That's great. Hey, did you hear about the steampunk festival this weekend? I was thinking about going on Saturday. Would you like to meet up with me?"

"Steampunk?" He raised an eyebrow; he did not know what she was talking about.

"It's a cosplay type of thing. People dress up like they walked off a spaceship from Victorian England. There will be some demonstrations, acting, vendors. I don't know much about it, but I've heard good things."

It could be a Renaissance fair or a pie-eating contest. It didn't matter, but if Tara wanted to spend time with him, he was going.

"I'm in. Tell me when and where."

CHAPTER FIVE

SATURDAY MORNING WAS an easier start to the Cogs and Corsets Steampunk Festival. Since the merchandise vendors' tables were inside the community building, they could be left in place overnight. Anna Lee had even felt safe leaving her items for sale in totes stashed under the table skirts.

She arrived an hour before opening to set out her merchandise. She had told Lauren to arrive at ten, but the responsible young lady had come thirty minutes early to help finish the setup.

"Good morning, Anna Lee. It's rather nice today; I wish we were outside."

"I agree, but it's a risk. It rained yesterday, and I was thankful to be sitting inside. Here, take these flower crowns and lay them on that table." Anna Lee pointed to the front table.

"Got it. And you're right about the weather. It's a risk. Did you have a lot of customers yesterday?"

"Yes, it was steady. I think today will be a little busier. Glad to have you here helping." Anna Lee tied on her apron, putting cash in the pocket for making change.

"I've heard about this festival but never been," Lauren replied. "I'm excited to be here to observe and learn."

Anna Lee glanced around. "Yes, and you can see how the vendors dress up and have a lot of fun! The people that come through are just as interesting. I enjoy just people-watching."

Visitors came into the vendor hall a few minutes early, and Anna Lee was thankful they were ready to go. They remained busy all morning. There was a lull around lunchtime, and she suggested Lauren take a break.

As soon as she walked away, a woman stopped by to browse the flower crowns on display. Anna Lee's breath caught when the woman looked up and smiled at her. She had a slight gap between her front teeth, just like Gene's. Anna Lee reminded herself that she couldn't start imagining the daughter she'd given up for adoption in every biracial woman she saw. She rubbed her thumb up and down the middle finger on her right hand, a nervous habit she could not break.

"Hello. Are you enjoying the festival?" she asked the woman.

"I am. It's been an eye-opening experience. I love these! I love that they're fresh flowers, not fake." She picked up a crown of light pink roses and lavender ribbon.

"Some people may think they're impractical, but I don't see how you can go wrong with the real deal. I'm Anna Lee. I own the In Bloom Flower Shop."

The woman held out her hand. "It's lovely to meet you, Ms. Anna Lee. I'm Ramona. I'll take two of the crowns. My nieces will love them. We're having a birthday party for them this afternoon. I was hoping to find something fun and unique here today, and these crowns are perfect."

"How old are your nieces?"

"Five. Twins. They are terrific girls. Fun and full of life, like all five-year-olds should be."

The customer completed the purchase and strolled away. Anna Lee thought about the nieces and hoped they would enjoy their crowns.

Nica, the young woman Anna Lee had recently hired at In Bloom, stopped by to chat with Anna Lee about the booth setup. Anna Lee had told her she wanted some sort of interesting booth setup for craft and vendor fairs like this. Nica wanted to get some ideas for this festival and was also thinking about flexibility, as Anna Lee needed the design to work for various festivals. Nica promised she would stop by later in the week to share a couple of sketches with Anna Lee.

Shortly after Nica left, Lauren returned with a salad for each of them. They ate quickly and readied themselves for the afternoon rush.

Thirty minutes before closing time, the crowd had thinned, and Anna Lee told Lauren it was time to pick up. They would leave two of each type of product out, and if someone was interested in something but wanted a different color, they could dig through the boxes for the desired color.

A man approached. He wore black slacks and a button-down shirt in a pale blue checked pattern. His brown hair was deep silver at the temples and salted with gray throughout the rest. He picked up a top hat that Anna Lee had adorned with a pair of aviator goggles, several small gold cogs, and two purple feathers that extended even higher than the hat.

"Well, what would they say at the office if I wore this on Monday?" he asked Anna Lee with a bright smile. The wrinkles around his eyes deepened, and Anna Lee felt like she was talking to an old friend, not a stranger browsing vendor booths.

Anna Lee laughed. "They would say you were a dapper gent with a pinch of whimsy."

He put the hat on his head and threw his arms out. "It's me, isn't it?"

"The hat makes the man."

"You approve?" he asked.

"I approve."

"Then I'll take it."

"Wonderful. You may just be my last sale of the day."

"That should make me memorable."

"Are you kidding?" Anna Lee put her hand on her hip. "With that hat on, I'd never forget you."

He laughed, a deep, comfortable laugh that warmed Anna Lee's soul. "Good, I like to be memorable." He pulled out his wallet. "How was business this weekend?"

Anna Lee told him the cost of the hat and answered, "Wonderful. I love coming to events like this where I can see so many people. It's exciting."

He looked down at the banner in front of her table. "In Bloom. I know that shop. It's in that old gas station, right?"

"Yes, it is."

"Great location and a unique building."

"Have you ever been inside?" Anna Lee was proud of how she had transformed the building from a dilapidated gas station and automotive repair station into a beautiful retail space and flower shop.

"Can't say I have. I've always had my secretary order flowers and what-not when needed."

Anna Lee considered that for a moment. He had a secretary that ordered flowers, not a wife. "Well, if your secretary doesn't order from me, I think she should."

"To be honest, I don't know where she orders from. I'll have to ask. From what I see here, you do incredible, creative work."

"Thank you."

Lauren walked up. "Should I take boxes out to the van?"

"Yes, dear. Use the wagon. It's under that table over there."

"Got it."

"Your daughter?" the man asked.

"Oh, no. No kids. Besides, she's young enough to be my granddaughter." Anna Lee turned away. Addressing questions about children was never easy. She hated that it felt like a lie. No, she hadn't raised kids, but she *had* had one. It was complicated.

"Forgive my assumption. But she's beautiful, just like you. An honest mistake."

"She is a beautiful young lady. She's smart, and she works hard, too."

"I'm sure you're all those things as well."

Anna Lee was thankful it was the end of the day, and there were very few people still milling about. It was nice having a conversation with this good-looking man who seemed to flirt with her. "I'm sorry. I didn't catch your name. I'm Anna Lee Foster." She held out her hand to shake his.

"I apologize. Talking your head off without a proper introduction. I'm John Peerson. It's very nice to meet you, Ms. Foster."

"Miss Foster."

He smiled, and it was like a hole opened in the roof of the building and a ray of sunlight illuminated the space around them even though they were still inside the building. An image of a spaceship beam flashed through Anna Lee's mind.

He put his hand out to shake hers. "My day can't get any better." He held her hand for several seconds longer than necessary. "Well, I can see you are ready to close. Can I give you a hand?"

"No, thank you. Lauren and I will make quick work of this. But I appreciate the offer."

"My pleasure. Well, I'll see you around, Miss Foster. I know where you work." He gave her a charming wink.

"Yes, you do. Have a great evening, Mr. Peerson."

He left just as Lauren returned. "That was a handsome gentleman. That was at least the third gentleman of a certain age that has flirted with you today."

Anna Lee brushed it off. "Men just waltz in and waltz out. That's fine by me."

Lauren raised an eyebrow. "I don't know. One of these days, someone is going to waltz in and not leave."

"That love stuff is for you young people. I'm too old to fall in love."

"I don't think so. Never too old for love."

"What about you? Any special person in your life?" Anna Lee gladly changed the trajectory of the conversation.

"No. I'm too busy. I don't want to meet someone right now."

"What happens if you meet someone while you're traveling overseas?" Anna Lee pulled the last tablecloth off and folded it neatly before putting it in a crate.

"That wouldn't be so bad. I hope to move to Europe, after college, of course. I hope to find a role in a large international company. Would be great to travel the world, running a large division."

"You keep dreaming big, Lauren. I'm rooting for you. Now, that's everything. These tables belong to the festival, so there is no need to load them up. Thank you again. Appreciate your support today. I'll see you next week. It's Saturday night; I'm sure you have some big plans."

"Not really. I'm staying in tonight to study. I'll see you on Thursday. Take care!"

ARRIVING HOME AFTER the festival, Salty informed Anna Lee that he was hungry with a loud "me-ow!"

After feeding the cat, Anna Lee poured a cup of chamomile tea, grabbed the pile of mail and her journal off the dinette, and walked to the front room. She sat on the couch, which gave her a view of the budding trees in the front yard.

She arranged her things, took the phone off the end table, setting it beside her. She knew she was one of the last ones on her block with a corded home phone, but she appreciated that it never needed to be charged.

She dialed her cousin Tabitha, who answered on the fourth ring.

"Yes?" Tabitha squeaked into the phone.

"Tabitha? It's me. What're you doing?" Anna Lee reached for the tea and eased back into the couch cushions, hoping this would be a long chat.

"Cleaning up from supper. Thinking about watching a movie. What are you doing?"

"Trying to stay awake until bedtime. Worked at a festival today and was on my feet the entire time. Even with compression socks, my feet are killing me."

Tabitha let out a soft grunt, and Anna Lee imagined the other woman sitting at her kitchen table. "Told you you're getting too old to keep that up, Anna Lee. It's time to retire! Enjoy yourself while you can. Won't be long until all the ailments hold us back."

"Speak for yourself. I plan to sky dive when I'm ninety." Anna Leer rolled her shoulders. She couldn't imagine having the physical capability to skydive at ninety.

Tabitha laughed, her voice dry and raspy. "I hope I'm around to see it."

Anna Lee thought back to their lunch last week and the dating discussion. "So, did you go out with your neighbor yet?"

"I did," Tabitha said, and Anna Lee could hear the smile in her voice. "We went to dinner and a movie last night."

Anna Lee chuckled. "Just like teenagers. How was it?"

"It was nice. No sparks though." Her voice quieted. "It was weird. I kept looking over his shoulder, looking for his wife. I'm not used to him being a widower yet, I guess. But I got out there and tried it. That's the important thing. Have you given it any more consideration?"

Anna Lee thought about the handsome man she'd met today, John Peerson. She'd felt a spark of interest. But was it worth it to try? Get herself out there like Tabby?

"Naw," she said. "Not a lot of eligible men cross my path, working in a flower shop."

"Well, maybe if you *retired*," Tabitha emphasized, "you'd have time to get out and meet people. Join a bridge club. Get back to church. There are ways to meet people."

"Volunteer at a senior care center," Anna Lee shot back. "Find a man in a wheelchair."

"You're old, not dead, cousin. Hey, my other line is ringing. Looks like it's Sam. I better get it in case he needs something."

They said goodbye and hung up.

She returned the phone to the end table and curled her feet up on the couch, rubbing the bunion on her left foot. Tabitha's comment about retiring came back. If she retired, she would have more time to work in her garden and make things. There were a few garden shows around the state she'd wanted to attend, but never could because of work.

If only I had a plan for the shop after I retire. If I could train someone in the business. Always hoped someone would work for me and would be interested in taking it over. Tilly's the only one who's ever shown a real interest in the shop. She likes to do things beyond her job description. She's got gumption; I love that. She doesn't have a planned career path yet, but she's young. Sometimes she says she's just in college to find a husband. I think she's kidding about that...

Placing the cup of tea on the coffee table, she picked up her journal and a pen.

April 7—I'm exhausted. Will keep this short. Steampunk Fest today. What a gas. The costumes, the people. Had a ball.

Met a handsome man. John Peerson. Nice. Funny. Good-looking. Thought about Tab's encouragement to date. Maybe she's right. What else am I going to do when I retire? Get another cat and become a crazy cat lady?

Maybe it is time to think about retiring. The workdays are getting harder. I can get through the day, but when I come home, there's not much left.

If I retired, maybe I could travel. I always wanted to but never had the chance. I would love to see all fifty states. Well, forty-nine. No way am I getting on a plane and flying over an ocean. That's rubbish. I'll only go where I can get there by land.

I'm not a fan of driving. Maybe I could talk Tabby into driving—she's more comfortable behind the wheel. We could road-trip! We could be like Thelma and Louise and have an adventure. Well, not exactly like Thelma and Louise; would like to make it home.

We probably couldn't drive out west or too far east. We could hit the Midwestern states—Wisconsin, Indiana, Michigan, Ohio. That would be a good start.

Having a gentleman to travel with would be nice. Safe.

Well, it's only seven-thirty, but I'm taking a bath and I'm crawling into bed. Might not get out of bed until Monday. If Salty will let me.

December 16, 1968–There is a new boy in my history class. He is so outrageously handsome. His family just moved here from Tennessee, and he has that southern drawl that makes my heart skip to my Lou. The teacher asked him what his three favorite things are, and he said "nature, listening to music, and making things"–those are all my favorite things too!

His name is Gene Powell. After the teacher introduced him, he sat at the desk behind me. I was so nervous that I'd do or say something stupid. After class, I stood and introduced myself to him. He shook my hand, and I felt a flash of electricity shoot up my arm. He looked at me with surprise, like he hadn't expected anyone to speak to him.

He's tall, at least six feet. Broad shoulders. He didn't slouch, stood tall, like he was daring someone to give him a hard time. He had a sweet smile and a dimple in one cheek. His eyes were friendly and warm. I think he had a scar on his forehead, but it could have been the lighting. I'll try to look closer tomorrow.

He's African American, but I don't care. My grandma always said when you close your eyes, you can't see the color of someone's skin. It doesn't matter. Of course, it might matter to my parents, but they can't rule my whole life. I'm getting too far ahead of myself. He probably wouldn't even find someone like me attractive. I'm too skinny and underdeveloped. I look more like a boy than a girl.

But if he did look at me, I'd look right back.

CHAPTER SIX

SUNDAY MORNING, JOHN woke a little earlier than usual and whistled as he showered and dressed. He was looking forward to talking to his daughter Kelley and telling her about the interesting woman he'd met at the steampunk festival. Her charm and wit had captivated him. When he'd gotten close enough to see her dark brown eyes, he'd felt comforted, at ease. He found her intriguing and wanted to get to know her better.

To pass time before he could call his daughter, he ran to the grocery store and the car wash, then picked up a newspaper before heading home.

The morning felt a little warmer than usual. The people he encountered seemed to be excited about the beautiful spring morning, and everyone was pleasant to each other. John wondered if the entire world had awakened in a good mood that morning or if it was just him. He was curious to see how his daughter sounded when he phoned her.

Once he felt it was late enough for her to be up, he called and waited patiently for her to answer. She did with a hushed, "Good morning."

He lowered his voice to match her volume. "Morning, hon. Why are we whispering?"

She laughed softly. "One sec."

He heard a door close on her end of the line and then she came on louder than before. "Sorry about that. I was peeking in on Maggie. Still sleeping, but her stuffy had fallen on the floor, so I was tucking it back in with her when you called."

"The ringer didn't wake her?"

"No," Kelley answered. "My phone was on vibrate and in my back pocket, thankfully. So, how are you doing this morning, Dad?"

"Fine. It's a beautiful morning."

"Same here. I am hoping we can go to the zoo today. It's too nice to be cooped up."

"That sounds wonderful." John thought Kelley seemed chipper today as well. Good, it wasn't only him. He wondered how long he could ask about Kelley before sharing his news. "How's Alex? The kids? You?"

"We're all good, Dad. Living the rat race. Trying to find balance. You know. How are things in Bloomington? Have you talked to my sisters lately?"

"I had dinner with Tara last week. Haven't talked to Deana in a while. Is she OK?" His heart jumped asking the question.

"As far as I know. I feel like I'm the odd girl out. They hardly ever call. They say they worry I'm busy with the kids, and they don't want to disturb me. It ticks me off. I am busy. Too busy to call them. They should call *me*."

John nodded his head, though Kelley couldn't see him. The girls had all left the house over eight years ago, but he was still refereeing their arguments. "Do you want empathy or solutions?"

Kelley grunted. "Both! Always." She paused, and he could hear the smile in her voice when she continued. "I don't mean to lay my frustrations with my sisters at your feet. But what advice do you have?"

"Perhaps you could text them and say, 'Hey, putting the kids down now, I'm free for the next two hours if you can talk.' Do that a few nights a week, and I bet you might hear from one or both. Or schedule a Zoom call when you're all available. Everyone's doing that these days."

"Right, we did that during lockdown with you. I kind of miss our Zoom family dinners."

"Maybe we should start that back up. Or at least I could get Tara and Deana here, and then we can get on Zoom with you."

"And have all three of you talking over each other? That sounds like a nightmare. I like the idea about family Zoomies, though, each from our own place. Maybe a Sunday evening thing."

John chuckled. "Lockdown or no lockdown. Let's do it. I marvel sometimes, wondering what your mother would have thought about the pandemic. Sometimes I'm thankful she missed it. She would have worried too much."

"She might have, but I wish she'd at least had the chance to be here."

"Yeah, I do, too." He regretted bringing up Margaret before telling Kelley about meeting the flower lady. Thankfully, Kelley opened the door for him.

"So, what's new with you?" she asked. "How was dinner with Tara?"

"Yes, we had a lovely…I guess you would call it dinner. Though I had to run home and eat a bag of potato chips, I was so famished afterwards."

Kelley laughed. "Where did you go?"

"A new gastropub. All the rage, per Tara. Tiny portions. I'm not sure it's legal to call it a meal."

"That's hilarious. Did you tell Tara you were thinking about dating again?"

"Yes, but…she's still not for it. But interestingly…" he trailed off.

"Yeah?"

"She invited me to a festival yesterday and when we separated while shopping, I met someone. Someone…intriguing."

"Yeah? That's great! Did you ask this someone out?"

"No. I just met her."

"Did you get her number at least?"

"No. Didn't do that either."

"Oh, no!"

"All is not lost. I know where she works."

"Whew! I thought this story went from outstanding to tragic in a flash. Well, are you going to go see her again? Maybe ask her out?"

"Yes, I think I'll do that." The thought made his heart race. He hoped Anna Lee wouldn't turn him down; he'd love to get to know her better.

"That's great. And ignore Tara. She's the baby being a baby. You've got to live your life. I'd feel better knowing you weren't lonely all the time. Mom would want it, too."

"I hope you're right."

"You know I am. Mom loved you. She'd want you to be happy. Oh, shoot. Joshua woke up and says he's starving. I better whip up breakfast. Love you, Dad! Talk soon!"

She hung up as soon as he said goodbye. John chuckled as he put the phone down on the table. The talk was what he'd needed. He wasn't looking for permission from his girls but knowing that at least one of them was all right with the idea eased a little of the anxiety he was feeling. He looked at the calendar and decided he was going to go for it. This week. He searched online for the business hours of In Bloom and saw that the store was closed on Mondays. He'd go on Tuesday.

TUESDAYS WERE USUALLY quiet at In Bloom. Anna Lee used the slow pace to place orders for flowers, supplies, or goods that she sold in the retail store. She liked to browse supply catalogs and magazines for inspiration. She also clipped pictures and articles that she wanted to keep and organized them in an accordion file folder that was easy to carry back and forth between the store and home.

Today, Salty was curled up in the front window, enjoying the spring sunshine upon his fur. Anna Lee was standing behind the counter flipping through a supply catalog.

She glanced at the clock. Only thirty minutes before she could close and go home. She glanced around the store to see if there was anything urgent that needed doing before she left. Finding nothing, she perched on the stool, put the catalogs away, and gathered the day's sales receipts from the coffee can.

"Salty, it's about time to go home. I bet you're looking forward to dinner. I know I am." She shoved the receipts into the bank bag under the register and tapped on the counter with her pinkie. She thought about her plans for dinner, baked chicken breast in a Tuscan herb sauce with veggies, and remembered that she needed to grab her planner out of the office so she could plan the rest of the week's meals. As she started towards her office to get it, the front door opened, and the bell jingled.

Turning around to offer assistance, Anna Lee was shocked to see John Peerson enter.

"Hello, Miss Foster," he said. She noticed the bunch of wildflowers that he held in his hand.

Salty stood and stretched at the stranger's entrance.

Anna Lee took a step back, and her initial shock eased. Her face softened into a smile as she realized she was thrilled to see John again. "Well, what a surprise. I thought your secretary ordered all your flowers."

"I wanted to let you know she was ordering from another florist, but she will order from In Bloom from now on. And I wanted to bring you these. I thought you might enjoy some simple roadside flowers." He dropped his gaze to the bouquet, looking back at Anna Lee with an uncertain smile. "Though I must confess, I don't know much about flowers. I hope I didn't pick any poison ivy."

Anna Lee approached and gazed at the bouquet. It was so pretty and vibrant, it reminded her of warm days and long walks. "Nope. No poisons. This here is Golden Alexander—it's a great pollinator—and this light purple flower is Wild Geranium, another great pollinator, and this bright purple one is Woodland Phlox."

"What you're saying is, I stole flowers that the bees need. I'm a jerk."

"Let me ask you this. Did you take all of them?"

"No, definitely not. These were plentiful. I only took a few of each."

"Then you're fine." She reached out and patted his arm. "I'm impressed that you remember the link between the flowers and the bees. Few people do these days. Which is apparent, with all the environmental issues we're having." She stopped babbling and smiled at John. "I appreciate the flowers; that was sweet of you. Can't remember the last time someone brought *me* flowers. I think it's the old adage of the cobbler's kids having no shoes." She took the bouquet from John and glanced around for a container. "Hmm, I have the perfect container in my office. Hold on a minute."

She took the flowers to the office and grabbed a white pitcher from a shelf. It was used for celebrations with the girls—birthdays, graduations, and going-away parties. She hated the going-away parties, but she hosted them with a big smile. It meant the girls were moving on with their lives and their careers.

She put a small glass upside down in the pitcher's bottom. Some flowers had short stems and would fall inside without the extra lift. She filled the pitcher with water and walked back to the front of the store.

John was looking at the table of birdhouses when she returned.

"You have a lot of interesting items. Not only flowers," he remarked.

"I have the space and wanted to have more than just flowers." She placed the pitcher of wildflowers on top of the counter and twisted it to find the right angle.

"More revenue streams."

"Sure, that too."

"How long have you been in business?"

"On my own, for over thirty years. I worked for an amazing florist in East Peoria for ten years before that. Learned about running a business. Learned the craft of flower arrangement. Then this building became available, and it called to me."

"It's an unusual building."

"It is! An old Standard Oil Gas Station. Closed in the sixties and sat empty for years. Came on the market in the late eighties, and I jumped on the opportunity. Took a couple years to restore it. Of course, I was still working full-time while I did that. Drove back and forth most days. Was here all day on my days off. But I had the vision, and I was much younger then."

She glanced around and shook her head at the memories. "I'm sure you didn't come by to hear me reminisce. What can I do for you, Mr. Peerson?"

He smiled. "Please call me John."

"Then you'd better call me Anna Lee."

He held out his hand, and she took it. "Deal," he said.

She laughed. "Deal."

His expression turned more serious. "I wanted to report back on our flower-ordering habits. That's done. I wanted to bring you some flowers to brighten your day. That's done. I hope they brightened your day."

She nodded.

He continued. "And last, I would like to ask you out to dinner. Friday night?"

Her head jerked involuntarily. "You're asking me out?"

"Yes."

"Why?"

"People do that when they are interested in other people. When they're attracted to other people."

Anna Lee was silent. Attraction? Interest? Her? It had been decades since she'd been on a date. She did not know what to expect. Her walls were built up, and she didn't think there was a reason to tear them down.

"I don't know what to say," she responded, her eyes darting from John to the floor, to the window, and back to John. She took a small step backward. "I don't drive after dark."

"You wouldn't have to drive. I'll pick you up. I noticed on the sign in your front window that you close at five on Friday. Could I pick you up at six-thirty? I was thinking we'd go to dinner. Get to know each other a little better. Good food. Pleasant conversation. No pressure."

What would she say if one of the young ladies that worked for her asked for advice? She would say, "You only live once"; "Go for it"; "Take risks. Life goes by too quickly." Could she take her own advice?

"Friday night. Dinner and conversation sound lovely; thank you for the invite. I have to say I'm out of practice with the dating thing. Please tell me if I make any for pars."

He smiled. "Do you mean *faux pas*?"

"Yep. Sure. Thought I'd start with a mispronunciation to see what you'd say."

"Well, did I pass?" he asked.

"With flying colors. Let me write down my address for you, and I'll see you Friday night."

Anna Lee had no idea where this was going, but she was excited about the possibilities.

CHAPTER SEVEN

ANNA LEE WAS thankful to have company in the shop on Thursday afternoon. Tilly and Lauren were helping with centerpieces for a birthday celebration that evening. It was a beautiful day, and Anna Lee had opened the garage bay door to let in fresh air while they worked. Salty was curled up inside the door, lying in a beam of sunlight. Anna Lee was confident he wouldn't go far if he woke and stretched his legs outdoors.

Anna Lee, listening to the girls talk about their plans for the weekend, wondered if she should bring up her own date.

Tilly's laugh brought Anna Lee back to the conversation. "My parents are going to be surprised when I show up on Sunday unannounced. I originally told them I couldn't make it to brunch because I have a paper due on Monday, but I finished the paper last night."

"Oh, they're going to love that!" Lauren exclaimed. "Is Kyle going with you?"

"No, he can't go. He has to work. I'll go solo."

"Are you driving there and back in one day?" Anna Lee asked.

"Yes. That's the downside of surprising them. If I wasn't doing that, I would drive up Saturday night and spend the night at home."

"Well, be careful," Anna Lee warned. "That's a lot of driving in one day. Will it be five hours in the car?"

"About that. It's Sunday; there shouldn't be a lot of traffic. It's a quick turnaround; I won't stay all day and drive back at night. I should be back here by four or five." Tilly tilted her head and shrugged her shoulders.

"That's good. Remember to pull over or call someone if you get drowsy."

Tilly was nodding before Anna Lee finished. "I will!"

Anna Lee turned towards Lauren and pointed out that she needed another bunch of greenery in her arrangement. "And what are you doing this weekend, Lauren?"

"Oops," Lauren replied, turning her compote bowl around and looking at the bare spot Anna Lee had pointed out. "Got it. Um, I don't have any special plans. I thought about going to see a foreign film that's showing in the student center. Like Tilly, I'm ahead in my studies, and I have some down-time this weekend."

"I can't imagine you ever being behind in class work. You're so well-organized. I need a few pointers," Tilly whined.

Lauren chuckled. "I'd be happy to help you with organizing your study habits. I'm happy with my system. Let me know when you have a couple of hours available, and I can come over and see what you're doing. Help if I can."

"That would be amaze-balls!" Tilly shouted.

Anna Lee shook her head. Being around these young ladies kept her on her toes.

"Well," she started, "I have plans this weekend." She paused for dramatic effect. "I have a date!"

Enjoying the look of shock on their faces, she chuckled to herself as she put another rose in the centerpiece she was working on. She fluffed the greenery and spun the vase around. Perfect. Getting up, she put the finished vase on the side table and waited for one of the girls to speak. She noted the round eyes they exchanged with each other.

"What?" Tilly finally exclaimed. "A date? You've never talked about dating before! I'm excited, don't get me wrong. I'm just shocked!"

Lauren echoed Tilly's surprise.

Anna Lee chuckled. "Not as shocked as I was when he asked me!"

"Well, spill! Who are you going out with? How do you know him? How did he ask you out? We have questions!" Tilly was practically bouncing in her seat.

Anna Lee grabbed another vase and brought it back to the worktable. As she sat down, a car drove up to the front of the portico and parked. "Ah, saved by the customer. I'll go take care of this and answer your questions when I come back."

Both girls groaned as Anna Lee made her way back to the retail space. The man waiting said that he needed a dozen red roses for a fifth anniversary gift for his wife. Anna Lee helped him choose the flowers and a card and rang up his purchases.

Returning to the garage bay, she noticed Salty had moved from his place by the open door to the worktable, where he was being petted and getting love from Tilly.

"All right. Are we done for the day?" Anna Lee asked.

"No. Not yet. Besides, you were getting ready to give us all the scrumptious details about your date. Even if we *were* done, we wouldn't be leaving!" Tilly replied.

Anna Lee sat on her stool and grabbed a handful of roses from the bucket on the table. "Oh, right. That. Well, you saw him, Lauren. The man that came up late Saturday at the festival."

"Oh! The man who bought the top hat!"

"Yes, that's the one."

Lauren looked at Tilly. "Yes, he was handsome. And he looked like a banker or businessman. Pressed clothes. Black slacks, if

I remember correctly. He looked a little out of place with the steampunk crowd."

"That's the one." Anna Lee began placing roses in the vase in front of her. "He came in here Tuesday night. Brought me the wildflowers that are on the counter."

"I wondered about those," Tilly said. "I couldn't recall you having flowers there before. It's a sweet touch."

"I thought so, too," Anna Lee said. "I might have to do that more often. Anyway, he came in and asked me out."

"When are you going?" Lauren asked.

"Tomorrow night."

"Well," Tilly said, "maybe you should take Saturday off. If it's a light day, we could handle it. And then you wouldn't have to worry if Friday night goes late."

"Oh, please. It's a first date and I'm old. I don't expect a late night. Besides, there is a wedding on Saturday. It won't be light."

Tilly raised her eyebrows, pursed her lips, and nodded. "Uh, huh. Well, we'll see. I'm excited for you and can't wait to hear all about it!"

September 13, 2021–Hired a new girl today. Matilda Miller. She goes by Tilly. Sweet young lady, bubbly and outgoing. She's a talker! She talked about the weather, restaurants within a three-block radius of the store, the ISU football schedule. She couldn't get enough of Salty—I thought the girl was gonna run off with my cat!

I've never seen a girl talk so much. Normally, that would put me off, but there was something about her. I felt a genuine connection with her in no time. Though she's nearly fifty years younger than me, it felt like we were fast friends. Never felt that with someone I've interviewed before. It was very strange. The interview flew by, and we were still talking about extraneous stuff. I didn't ask any of my normal questions.

Don't matter, I could tell by the way she dressed and carried herself that she has an eye for beauty. She had on a coneflower blue shift dress with a matching shrug and heels. She could have been interviewing for a job at the phone company. And she could talk to anyone. She'll do great in the store, helping customers.

I bet she has to shoo the boys away. Seems like she'd attract 'em like flies to a cow patty. She starts next week.

I smell my banana bread. Better grab it before it burns.

CHAPTER EIGHT

ER DOORBELL RANG at six-thirty on the dot. At the door, Anna Lee smoothed down her long purple dress and took a deep breath. "You can do this, lady," she told herself before opening the door.

John stood on the porch wearing a black suit with a white shirt and blue tie. The top hat that he had purchased from her on Saturday sat jauntily on top of his head.

He held a small bunch of wildflowers. It looked like the same assortment that he'd brought to the flower shop.

"Hello," she said, smiling. "Nice hat. Are you going to wear that to dinner?"

John bent over slightly, touching the hat. "Good evening, Miss Foster. You look lovely this evening."

"Cut the formality, John. Would you like to come in? Will we be late for our dinner reservation?" Anna Lee waved him in and hoped he didn't see the slight shake in her hand.

"We have a little time. I made reservations for seven, and it will take us ten minutes to get there."

"Are you going to tell me where we're going, or keep me guessing?"

"Let it be a surprise."

"Come in. Can I get you something to drink? I was debating opening a bottle of wine before you got here."

"I'm on an antibiotic. I can't drink tonight."

"What for?"

He looked down like a kid caught with his hand in the cookie jar. "Cut my leg when I was using the weed whacker on Sunday. Got a good gash. The doctor wanted to make sure it didn't lead to something else. Oh, and these are for you." He held out the bouquet.

Anna Lee took the flowers and turned towards the kitchen. "Goodness! I have nonalcoholic drinks, too. Come on into the kitchen."

She was glad she'd tidied up during the week. She had shoved a lot of current projects into the back room and shut the door, hoping she'd find what she was looking for when she needed it.

In the kitchen, she gestured towards the table and told John to take a seat. She bustled about putting the flowers in a blue mason jar and getting iced tea from the refrigerator. Setting both on the dinette, she went to the cupboard for glasses.

John sat at the table and put the top hat on the seat next to him. "You have a lovely, lively home. It suits you perfectly."

"Thank you. I love it," she said as she poured tea. "Though I sometimes feel like I'm rattling around in a house that's way too big for me. But that's what you get when you're single and move into a four-bedroom Victorian. These houses were built for large families. But I fell in love with it the moment I saw it. The garden, the brick driveway, the turret. Everything I wanted in a house."

She sat down at the table and took a drink of the tea. *Everything except a family*, she thought.

John seemed to read her mind. "But you never married? No kids?"

"That's a story for another time. If I tell you all my secrets now, you won't take me out for a nice dinner." Moving the spotlight off herself, she asked, "What about you? The basics. Marital status. Family. Go."

John smiled. "I'm a widower. Lost my wife, Margaret, five years ago. We have three beautiful daughters. Kelley is the oldest. She's thirty-four. She's married to Alex, and they have a son and a daughter. Next is Deana, she's thirty-one. Engaged. Will get married next spring. And my youngest is Tara. She dates, but no serious relationship."

"Sounds like a wonderful family. I'm sorry about your wife. How did she die?"

"Breast cancer. It was a beast." He leaned back in his seat and clasped his hands together tightly. "The treatment is as bad as the disease. I was going to retire at sixty-five; I was sixty-two when she got sick. We were looking forward to my retirement. We had a lot of plans. Once she passed, I decided to keep working. Staying busy seemed to help with the grief. The girls were all out of the house when she died. I helped them with their grief as much as I could. They held *me* up most of the time."

Anna Lee reached out and touched his clasped hands. "They sound like amazing women. You and your wife did good raising them. There's something you can be proud of. Your wife must have been a wonderful lady."

"She was. Thank you for saying that." He sighed and looked at his watch. "We should be on our way. I would love to spend all evening right here chatting, but I'm also hungry. I hope you are, too."

"Famished. Let's go." They exchanged smiles, and Anna Lee felt the evening was off to a great start.

DINNER WAS DELIGHTFUL. The conversation flowed easily. John was a skilled communicator and had lots of stories to share about his travels and work.

Anna Lee studied his features during dinner. His hair was well-trimmed. His eyes were blue-green and reminded her of lake water. When she was a young child, her grandparents' home was on a lake. Her family visited every summer weekend to swim, fish, and picnic. That was before life got complicated.

For dessert, they each ordered gelato. John got the coffee flavor, and Anna Lee ordered chocolate with a caramel swirl.

After the server set their desserts down, John asked for the check and turned back to Anna Lee. "Are you ready to share your deepest secrets now? Will the gelato loosen your tongue?"

"If the Chablis didn't, the gelato will." Anna Lee took a bite and looked down at the dessert. Where to begin?

"I won't bore you with the nonessentials tonight. I guess it's good to come clean and let you decide if you're interested in seeing me anymore." She took a deep breath and set the gelato cup down. "I never married. I was deeply in love as a young woman. A teenager. Seventeen years old, and I thought I had found the love of my life. His name was Gene. It was the late sixties, and you could say we were star-crossed lovers. He was Black, and my parents didn't approve. It didn't matter to me. He became the single most important thing in my life. He was the sweetest, kindest man. He joined the Army and was sent to Vietnam. He didn't return home."

John softly murmured, "Oh, no".

She glanced at the gelato cup; the dessert was melting. Oh well, she couldn't stomach it now, anyway. She continued, "I was devastated, as you can imagine."

She looked up at John, and he had pushed his dessert aside, too. He reached across the table and waited for her to put her hand in his. She did, and he gently brushed his thumb across the top of her hand. It was a sweet gesture, and it felt good to place her hand, and her trust, in another person's. It had been a long time.

"You have to be strong to go through losing someone you love at such a young age," John said.

"I don't know about strong," she said. "I think it broke me. Broke an important part of me. I've never healed from it. It's prevented me from letting anyone get too close and from falling in love again."

She thought about the pregnancy and the baby she'd given up for adoption. She was not springing that on John on the first date. Those wounds ran deep and sharing the story with a near-stranger could rip the scars wide open. If he was repulsed by the decision she'd made more than fifty years ago, and why wouldn't he be, then all the pain and heartache would boil over and make a mess of her heart all over again.

"Finding a love like that can feel like a once-in-a-lifetime occurrence," John said, squeezing her hand and pulling back. "There was a time when I felt that way about Margaret. That she would be my one true love for all my life. I don't mean to say I love her any less now than I ever did. I love her as much as ever. But I found, after the grief subsided, that there was room in my heart for more love. And it doesn't take away my love for my wife. I think our capability to love is expansive. Like when our first daughter was born, I thought my heart couldn't handle any more love and joy. Then the next child comes along, and you see that there is plenty of room for more love."

John cleared his throat and rubbed his chin. Anna Lee thought his little speech was sweet, and it touched her to see him get emotional. He appeared to be buttoned-up and professional, from his short haircut to his smooth jaw to his suit. He looked as though he could have walked out of an office meeting before taking her to dinner.

She still felt like the long-haired hippie child of her youth. If she thought about it too long, she'd tell herself that they were complete opposites and had no business being together. Truth to be told, she found him charming and thoughtful.

"Well, I see our gelato has melted, and I think we've had enough heavy conversation for one evening. I'm too old to go three rounds on such heavy subjects," Anna Lee said, shifting in her seat.

John smiled and nodded. "You're right. Let me pay the check and I'll take you home. I hope the seriousness of the conversation didn't scare you too much."

"Nope. Good to get serious occasionally." Anna Lee smiled. This date was the best decision she had made in years.

THE RIDE HOME was too short. Anna Lee enjoyed the rich leather seats of John's car. He hit a button for a seat heater that warmed her chilled bones, and she snuggled back, marveling at the coziness she felt. Maybe she deserved a little luxury, once in a while. Even in a gas-guzzling automobile.

Dinner was perfect. John had listened to her story about falling in love with a Black man in the sixties without judgment and it was a balm to her heart's wounds.

On the drive back to her house, John explained where he lived, and she discovered his house was only a few miles from hers. It would be an easy scooter ride, lovely in the summer.

He told her, too, where he had found the wildflowers that he'd brought her, and she planned to visit the field soon to harvest seeds to plant in her own yard.

The car pulled up to the curb in front of her house much too soon. She blinked her eyes and looked up at the large house, noting that the trim needed to be scraped and painted again. She had done it herself the last time, almost eight years ago. Now she dreaded climbing the tall ladders to reach the second and third-story trim. If she fell, it would be all over. Even if she lived through the fall, the convalescence would be long and painful.

She feared needing a rehabilitation center; if she went in, would she come out?

"I'll come around and open your door. Give me one minute," John said, opening his own door.

Anna Lee smiled at the gentle gesture. She wondered if young men were still chivalrous these days.

Her door opened, and she shivered at the cool air that rushed in towards her. John held out his hand to her. She accepted it, eased her legs out, and stood with a little wobble as her toe caught the curb.

"I'm sorry, I parked too close," he said as his other hand came forward and grasped her waist to help steady her. "Easy, now."

"I'm fine. I'm fine. It's dark is all; I didn't see how close the curb was." She stepped up onto the grass and smiled at John. "Thank you. For the help getting out of the car, the lovely dinner, and the wonderful conversation. I haven't had a more pleasant evening in ages."

The glow from a streetlamp highlighted John's blue-green eyes. Anna Lee was close enough to make out little flecks of gold.

They started walking towards her front door, John's hand resting lightly on her lower back.

"Would you like to come in?" Anna Lee asked when they reached the stairs.

John followed her up the four steps. "I would love to, but I'd better not. I have a feeling we'd end up talking all night, and it would take me all weekend to recover."

Anna Lee tilted her head back and laughed. "You may be right. And I have a store to run tomorrow, and a wedding, to boot."

At the front door, she pulled her keys from her handbag and slid the right one into the lock. She turned to John before turning the key. "Again, thank you."

He reached for her hand and held it. She wanted to bottle the feeling that flowed through her from his touch, as if she was canning veggies to get her through a long, hard winter.

A smile started on the left side of his mouth and slowly spread. "It was my pleasure. Truly. Haven't felt this hopeful and excited since my wife passed away. I will treasure our evening together, and I can't wait to do it again. I hope you agree with me."

She smiled. "I agree."

"Good. Good. I know you are working tomorrow. Would it be all right if I call you tomorrow evening to check in, see how your day went?"

"There's nothing I'd like more," she replied, surprised to find she meant it.

"Wonderful. I will do that. Now, I hope you have a restful evening and a great day tomorrow."

Before Anna Lee could respond, John leaned forward and pressed his lips softly to her cheek. She closed her eyes and inhaled the warm, earthy scent of his aftershave. Her arms rose of their own accord and rested on his arms; she had the urge to wrap her arms around him and hold him close, but that would be too forward of her.

Too soon, he pressed his lips closer, sighed, and pulled back. His eyes met hers, and Anna Lee wanted to search the depths of his for something. She wasn't sure what, but she wanted to find an answer in his eyes.

Breaking the moment, she said, "Good night, John," and turned the key in the lock. John murmured his own good night and turned towards the street.

Stepping into the foyer, Anna Lee heard Salty meow in greeting and reproach. Without addressing the cat, she shut the door and leaned over to push aside the curtain in the sidelight. She watched John climb into his car. It didn't start right away, and Anna Lee imagined he was looking towards the house. She gave a small wave, not knowing if he could see her or not.

Dropping the curtain, she turned into the dark house. "Salty, do I have a story for you."

October 18, 1969–I thought it was a good thing that I'd gained some weight back, but I haven't been feeling good and everything upsets my stomach, so Mom sent me to the doctor. I thought it was just the continued stress of not knowing where Gene is, or if he's all right.

Turns out, I'm pregnant. Thank goodness Mom didn't go to the appointment with me. She would have caused such a scene. I asked the doctor to call her and give her the news for me, though. I couldn't tell her to her face. It was bad enough when I got home. She wouldn't look at me, she just sent me to my room.

I've tried to write a letter to Gene, but I just cried and cried, and the tears stained the paper. I'll write it when I can manage to do it without crying.

If I can get the support of our families, I think I can manage until he comes home. Then we can marry, and we'll raise the baby together.

After the initial shock, I'm sort of excited. I always wanted to be a mom. I thought marriage would come first, but it's ok if it comes after.

I know I shouldn't, but I hope it's a baby girl. I will learn how to knit so I can make her cute dresses and bonnets.

CHAPTER NINE

ON SATURDAY MORNING, Anna Lee drove to In Bloom on her scooter, Salty snug in the backpack behind her. She drove more slowly than usual, thinking about the date with John. She was looking forward to sharing an update with the young ladies at work and thinking about calling her cousin Tabitha to get her wise counsel.

At the store, she walked in through the back door, put the backpack down, and let Salty loose. He sauntered off to the front of the store and his favorite napping place in the window.

She performed all the opening routines: place money in the cash drawer, review the day's wedding event, and put on a pot of coffee.

Paige arrived first, and Tilly and Lauren ten minutes later. When the girls were sitting at the table, coffee in hand and a sample centerpiece in the middle, Anna Lee returned to the retail side to stock greeting cards. That job complete, she returned to the garage bay workroom and settled in to work on her first centerpiece.

The girls were talking about their classes and exams. Once the school talk ran its course, Tilly turned to Anna Lee and flashed a brilliant smile. "Anna Lee, don't think we forgot about your date. We want to hear all the details!"

Paige's forehead scrunched. "Date? What date?"

Lauren responded, "Anna Lee had a date last night. With a man she met at the steampunk festival last weekend."

"That's amazingly amazing!" Paige exclaimed. "Please spill, Anna Lee!"

Tilly jumped to her feet. "Wait! I need more coffee. Who else?"

Everyone said they could use a refill, and Anna Lee took a moment to think about what she would share.

Once the cups were filled, Anna Lee began. "I had a wonderful time. We hit it off. John—"

"John?" Paige repeated. "Aw."

Anna Lee smiled. "John was a gentleman."

"Does that mean no action?" Tilly asked.

"Definitely no action." Anna Lee shook her head, and her hair swished across her shoulders. "Sorry if that's all you wanted to hear."

Tilly sighed dramatically. "Not all. But I hope you got a goodnight kiss, at least!"

"There was a respectable goodnight kiss on the cheek."

The young ladies sighed in unison, and Anna Lee blushed.

"You know my generation doesn't kiss and tell. Anyway, it was a wonderful date. He was attentive, kind, and interesting."

"Are you going to go out again?" Paige asked.

"He hasn't asked me yet, but I think so."

"That's great!" Tilly said.

Anna Lee's smile widened; it *was* great. After putting up such a fuss when Tabitha suggested dating, she was surprised at how easy and fun the evening with John had been. Maybe she would have a good experience with dating this time around. One could hope.

It was time for a change of subject. She didn't want to ruin the joy she felt by talking too much about it. She needed to keep her excitement in check. If she wasn't careful, the fates might come and take it from her. "Paige, what are your plans for the rest of the weekend? I talked to Lauren and Tilly about theirs on Thursday."

Lauren jumped in. "Nice change of subject, Anna Lee!"

Paige laughed. "Studying and preparing for the week ahead. I also plan to do some research on things to do in New York City on the cheap. I want to get as much out of my summer internship as I can, and I'll need to watch my budget."

"You are going to have a wonderful time, and it's always good to mind your P's and Q's," Anna Lee said. "It's great to see you fulfilling your dream."

Tilly whined, "Paige is going to New York, Lauren is going to Europe, and I'm going crazy." She smiled. "Just kidding!"

"I'm glad you'll be here this summer, Tilly," Anna Lee said. "I've hired one new person for the summer and hope I don't need to add any more."

"I think this summer is going to have a lot of amazing surprises for all of us," Paige said.

Anna Lee couldn't agree more. Things were definitely looking up.

August 19, 2002–I knew I shouldn't have gone on that date. Note to self: never go out with a man that comes into the flower shop and asks me out. I need references or a background check. Would have been better use of my time to stay home and scrub toilets.

Won't make that mistake again.

On a related note, found a dead mouse in one of my traps. Seems a little early for them to be finding their way inside. Usually don't see them buggers until October.

CHAPTER TEN

THE FOLLOWING SATURDAY, there were no weddings or special events scheduled, so Anna Lee did something she had not done in years; she took the day off. John had called every day that week, starting the day after their first date, as promised. With each additional call, they got to know a little more about each other: their families, their histories, their likes, and dislikes.

She'd spent the morning planting flowers in her yard. The day was sunny, warm in the sunshine and cool in the shade. As she worked the soil, added fertilizer, and gently placed plants and flowers into the ground, the idea of a relationship, unfathomable a few short weeks before, grew on Anna Lee. She pictured it as a seedling needing water, food, light, and constant nurturing. The daily phone calls were becoming a ray of sunshine to her soul.

Most of the flowers planted—Rome wasn't built in a day, and her flower beds didn't need to be, either—Anna Lee stood, stretched, and lifted the hat from her head. Using the sleeve of her dress, she wiped the beads of perspiration from her brow.

She put her hands on her hips and flexed her shoulders, pushing her elbows back. The stretch felt good. She raised her face to the sun, letting the warmth on her face fuel her for the afternoon ahead.

She took her time putting her tools back into the small garage and started for the back door.

"Salty!" she cried. "Come on! Dinnertime!"

She opened the storm door that led to the back porch, and her eyes swept the backyard, looking for the cat.

"I mean it, Salty! Come on, now! Or I'll lock this door and you'll have to find a poor little mouse for your dinner." She wondered what the neighbors thought of her threats.

Salty dashed out from underneath a hydrangea bush and darted up the steps. "I thought so," Anna Lee said, following the orange cat inside.

JOHN ARRIVED SHORTLY after one, which had given Anna Lee time to shower and clean up the kitchen. This visit, he knocked on the back door instead of ringing the bell for the front door. Anna Lee had told him that visitors who knew her, knew to come to the back, because she was usually in her backyard or in the kitchen when she was home.

She was standing at the kitchen sink when he knocked. Airing out the house with the fresh spring breeze, she had left the kitchen door open, allowing the breeze to blow through the screened back porch and into the kitchen.

"I brought the bread you asked for," John said, walking in with a bag of freshly baked bread, the warm smell wafting around him. She was making homemade vegetable soup, which would go well with fresh bread.

"You remembered," Anna Lee said, eyeing the loaf of French bread sticking out of his bag.

He stepped into the kitchen, and Anna Lee greeted him with a quick hug.

"Of course. How could I forget?" He set the bread on the counter.

"I hope you're hungry," she replied, heading back to the stove to stir.

Anna Lee wondered if John would expect her to give up her home if they decided to live together or even marry. She shook her head gently; it was too soon for those thoughts. No need to borrow trouble. That was a concern for another day.

"I am. What can I do to help?" he asked, glancing around.

"How about cuttin' up that bread?" Anna Lee pulled out a cutting board and pointed to the knife block on the counter. "The soup is ready. I'll set the table while you cut."

Once they sat at the table to eat, Anna Lee asked John about his daughters and how well they had dealt with their mother's illness.

"It was rough. In order to protect them, we did not share just how sick she was. They were all out of the house, so they didn't see the severity of the illness firsthand. They didn't see how the treatment ravaged her for days afterwards. I regret not sharing more. When I finally had to tell them there weren't many days left, they were shocked and angry. Rightfully so."

He took a deep breath. "I want to be completely open and honest with them from here on out."

Anna Lee reached out and placed her hand on his. She squeezed it quickly, then released it. "Always the best thing to do. How are they now?"

John lifted his eyes back up to meet hers and smiled. "They're fine. They are attentive to me and call a little more often than they used to."

"I bet you like the attention."

"Who wouldn't?" He laughed. "I appreciate that I've grown closer to each of them and regret not having made more effort before. Margaret spoke to at least one of them every day. Once they were older and out of college, I became obsessed with achieving all that I could at work. The girls needed their daddy less and less each day. I hate to admit I got my priorities messed up."

He paused, and Anna Lee let his words settle in. She smiled and hoped her presence comforted him. After a few moments, she nodded slowly. "I hear that. I've always thrown myself into work, into volunteering, into staying busy for the sake of it. Was easier than being self-reflective and questioning if I was living my life right."

"Sounds like we have one more thing in common." John lifted his soup bowl. "Do you mind if I get a bit more?"

"Please do." Anna Lee buttered another slice of the fresh bread while John was at the stove. She hesitated to bring up the next topic, but John wanted honesty. "When the time is right, I'd love to meet your family."

"I think the time is right, right now!" he said as he turned from the stove. "No time like the present, as they say. I think the girls will be happy I'm seeing someone—well, my oldest will be. The other two…" Shaking his head, he added, "Kelley asks me constantly if I'm dating." He smiled, and Anna Lee wondered if she'd ever get used to the way his smile made her feel. Giddy. Hopeful. Renewed.

She laughed at his response. "Well, if you don't think it's too soon…" Her voice trailed off. She didn't want to get ahead of herself here.

John sat down and reached for her hand. "Hey, you OK, there? You look troubled."

She sighed. It was nice to have someone who could read her emotions so quickly. "I'm all right. I'm excited about meeting your daughters. I just hope they'll like me. It's been a long time since I've been brought around to meet the family." She scoffed. "Heck, last time I was, it was to meet someone's parents, not their kids."

John's thumb moved softly across the back of her hand. "Well, don't worry. I don't need their approval; I am the dad, after all."

Anna Lee smiled. He had the right answer to her objections. She would stop worrying about it. She didn't want to live a life full of worry and regret.

AFTER JOHN LEFT, Anna Lee sat in her living room, working on a jigsaw puzzle, and drinking a cup of tea. She reflected on the afternoon spent with John as she finished the puzzle.

Once it was done, she went to the kitchen to get a glass of cold water with lemon. Closing the refrigerator door, she turned and noticed her journal on the dinette. She sat down and pulled it close to her.

April 21—What a wonderful Saturday. I took the day off and let Tilly run the shop, as there were no events today. That will change now that we're officially in wedding season. Weddings are booked every Saturday from now until September.

John came over today for lunch. He helped me in the yard, and we shared lots of stories about ourselves.

John told me all about his daughters and I cannot wait to meet them. He suggested a dinner with the two that live around here sometime. The one that's married lives in Chicago. She should be down in a few weeks with her kids. Would be wonderful to meet them.

I asked John if it was too soon to meet his family. He said life's too short to wait for anything at our age. I couldn't agree more.

I haven't felt this excited in decades. Life has been on autopilot for too long. Maybe there are a few more adventures waiting for this old broad yet.

May 10, 2014–Oh, what a day! I was working in the yard this afternoon, planting some tree peonies on the east side of the garage — found the prettiest peonies that are white with purple and gold in the middle — anyway, toward the back of the yard, I started hearing this little squeaky noise, thought at first it was a mouse, but turns out it was a little kitten, all alone. Poor thing seemed frightened out there by itself. Not sure what happened to its momma, it's probably just a couple of months old. Anyway, I brought it in, gave it some milk, and made a bed out of old towels on the back porch. Called a few vet offices today and have an appointment in the morning. If the little thing checks out all right, I think I'll keep it. It's a soft orange and white, reminds me of a cracker.

Always thought I'd eventually get a dog but hadn't got to it yet. A dog's usually more companionable than a cat and could be a protector. I've grown more fearful of being here all by myself. If someone tried to break in, I'd offer them the keys to save my life. Don't think I could fight anyone off, though I keep a baseball bat by the front door and by the back door, just in case. If I could take a swing on the offensive, I might do all right.

But this kitten found me. Guess it was fate. I wasn't looking for a pet. Not sure I could leave it alone when

I'm at work all day, could be eight or nine hours. It'd stress me out to think about him here all alone. If he stays, we'll figure something out.

He's lying in the middle of a towel and sound asleep on my lap right now. He's so adorable and soft, looks like an earmuff. Hope he doesn't have fleas. I'll kick myself for bringing him into the house if he does. I'll put him on the back porch overnight with a little heater out there, so he doesn't get too cold. If he checks out OK tomorrow, I'll make a bed in the corner of my bedroom.

He's purring, and it's the softest sound, can barely hear him over the refrigerator hum. The durn thing has my heart bursting with happiness. What's Tabby going to say when she finds out a cat adopted me? She's gonna say I done gone soft. Well, maybe she's right. Maybe I have. Only took me sixty-two years.

CHAPTER ELEVEN

THE SUN STREAMED in through In Bloom's large front window. Salty was taking advantage of the warmth as he napped, curled up in the corner of the window ledge. Anna Lee had replaced the small blanket on the ledge that morning with a clean one, putting the dirty one in a tote bag to take home and wash.

The bell over the door was mostly quiet; Wednesdays were typically slow. Anna Lee was keeping herself busy by knitting a baby blanket. The shelves were stocked, the orders placed, and she couldn't find anything else in the store to do. She kept a stash of yarn and extra knitting needles in the store for slow days like this.

She sat at the counter so she could watch the cars go by and be there if someone walked in. She wasn't too worried about the skeins of yarn taking up space on the counter. If a customer walked in, she could manage around the mess.

An hour of sitting and knitting had her backside aching. She got up and walked to the office to put on the kettle. It was time for tea.

Before the kettle whistled, she heard a truck slowly rumbling outside. She was expecting a delivery of vases and hoped the sound meant her delivery was here. She shuffled into the storefront, ready to direct the delivery man. As she looked out the door, she saw the truck pulling up and thought to herself that he seemed a little too close.

Since the building was an old gas station, there was a carport that allowed people to stay dry as they came in if it was raining. Though the gas pumps were no longer there, the curb still held the large pillars that held up the portico.

Her eyes widened, and she hastened across the floor. He was too close! He was going to hit a pillar!

Too late. There was a loud bang, and the building vibrated. Salty woke with a start, jumped off the ledge, and ran for the office. He would probably hunker down under the desk. Anna Lee assured herself he'd be safe there. She rushed to the counter, grabbed the cordless phone, and headed outside to assess the damage.

The front door opened with no issue. That was a good sign. When she got to the truck, the driver was exiting and looking at the post with dismay.

Luckily, his truck was lower than the roof, so there was no collision there. From Anna Lee's viewpoint, it looked like his front bumper had clipped the post. He'd come in too close.

"Are you all right?" she called as she neared him. She didn't recognize this driver. *Must be a newbie.*

"Yes, ma'am," he said, ducking his head. "Can't believe I hit it."

He walked around the front of the truck and looked at the impact site. "Man. My boss is going to kill me. It's my first day." He shook his head. His light blue eyes were large and round. He looked like he was going to cry or punch something.

"He can't kill ya," Anna Lee said. "That's illegal. We will have to report it, though. I'll call the police and have someone come out to write us a report. For insurance, you know."

"Right." He glanced at the roof over the walkway. "Do you think it's safe to stand here? The building's old."

"Old and sturdy. Like me," she quipped. "It's fine. But if it makes you nervous, you can move."

As the kid strolled over to the other side of the overhang, Anna Lee called the non-emergency hotline and asked for an officer to come file a report. Next, she called her insurance agent. Best to get him out here, too.

What a mess. She was thankful no one was hurt, but she worried that there might be structural damage. Hoping she wouldn't have to close the store for days or weeks while repairs were made, she sent a prayer heavenward.

It was times like these that she wished she had a partner. Not necessarily a partner in her business, but a life partner, a spouse or significant other. Someone she could call and vent to or ask to "come right away, I need help," for support, or a hug, whatever she needed. That would be nice.

HOURS LATER, ANNA Lee wondered how she was still on her feet. It had taken ages for the insurance adjuster to arrive, then he had to call an engineer out to decide if the building could be used while the work to repair the pillar was scheduled and performed.

After a healthy debate, they decided that the store should be closed while the work was done. The insurance agent promised he'd help her get it scheduled in the next couple of days.

For added precaution, the engineer requested that they place barriers around the front of the building to prevent cars from coming within ten feet of the damaged area.

Anna Lee called in reinforcements, namely Trevor Morrison, a plumber she knew well. He was strong and young, in his late twenties, she guessed. Trevor was a sweetheart, and he drove over as soon as he got off work. He brought two friends along with him, a kid named Hawk and another named Devonte. Anna Lee explained what needed to be done. Luckily, she had several large concrete planters in the backyard near the picnic area that they could carry to the front and place strategically at each end of the driveway next to the building.

Trevor ran to the lumberyard and bought a couple of metal park benches they put in front of two pillars holding up the overhang.

"That'll keep any cars from getting too close, Miss Anna Lee," Trevor said, gazing out the front window. His friends had already left.

The temperature dropped when the sun went down, and Anna Lee was staying inside, supervising the work.

"I can't thank you enough for coming quickly and bringing extra muscles," she said, nudging his arm with her shoulder.

"Glad we could help. What a crazy day you've had."

"Yeah. I'm worn out. Hate to drive home in the dark, too, but I'm ready to get home and get in bed. Suppose I should eat, too."

"I can drive you home."

"That's nice of you, but how would I get back here to get my scooter?"

She thought about John, but their relationship was too new to be calling him and asking for a favor.

"I'll pick you up in the morning."

"Naw, you have to be at work too early."

"I'll take a break and come get you. It's not a problem at all. Please let me do this. The way your day has gone, I wouldn't feel right letting you and Salty ride home on the scooter. You're likely to get run over. Don't put that on my conscience."

Anna Lee laughed. "You got that right. All right, I'll let you drive me. Appreciate the offer. I'll get the cat backpack, and we'll be ready."

She quickly wrote up a sign for the front door saying they were closed until Saturday. She changed the outgoing greeting on the answering machine to let customers know she wouldn't be in.

Those tasks completed, she picked up the backpack and moved the chair from under the desk. Salty was still cowering below the desk. "It's OK, ol' boy. We're going home now."

She opened the backpack, and Salty jumped in. She hoisted the strap over her shoulder and closed the office door. Grabbing the keys out of her dress pocket, she made the rounds, locking the doors, and met Trevor out front.

They were quiet as they drove to Anna Lee's house. She was too tired to make small talk, and Trevor didn't force it.

Once they were home, Salty devoured his dinner. They were home two hours later than normal, and the orange cat padded upstairs where Anna Lee knew he'd soon climb up on her bed and fall asleep. She didn't think he'd slept at all while he was hiding in the office, away from the commotion.

Anna Lee put a slice of bread in the toaster and poured herself a cup of milk. She thought about writing a few sentences in her journal, but it would wait for another day. She was going to eat, take a hot bath, and go to bed. Those were her priorities for tonight. She'd seen a missed call from John earlier. That was going to have to wait until tomorrow, too.

She leaned against the counter and sipped the milk. The events of the day had taken a toll on her, physically and mentally. "Maybe I am too old to keep this up," she said aloud to the empty room.

The day-to-day responsibilities were fine. She had no problem managing those. And she felt that working, staying busy, was what kept her going. She couldn't imagine being retired and not having something she had to do each day, like get to the store and open. Staying engaged kept her mind sharp and her joints moving. She worried that if she retired, she wouldn't be as active, and it would get harder to get around.

But then there were incidents like today's—an accident, something breaking, the risk of a customer getting hurt and suing her—that would take hold of her thoughts, and she'd worry about what-ifs. The stress of that worry would weigh on her, and the thought of being retired held a newfound interest for her.

August 3, 1978–Today was my first day working for Mr. And Mrs. Carrington at Frank's Flowers on SW Adams. I can't believe they gave me the job! I have no experience with flowers, but Mrs. Carrington said my experience waiting tables and working the register at Woolworth's prepared me for dealing with customers. Mrs. Carrington will teach me about flower design. I feel so lucky and excited to be given this opportunity and I'm not going to ruin it. I'm going to take lots of notes, and learn, and eventually I hope Mrs. Carrington will trust me enough to design my own arrangements. Shouldn't put my cart before the horse, but I know this is right for me.

I love flowers. Always have. My grandma had the prettiest garden. Mom does too, but it's been so long since I've been home, it's fading from my mind. Not sure why I can remember grandma's house so clearly. She had the loveliest rose bushes. I learned the hard way not to get too close. But to get my nose close to the flowers and inhale…I could do it for hours, practically drunk off the scents.

Surprisingly, Mrs. Carrington didn't turn up her nose to see that I have a GED instead of a high school diploma because I went to the maternity home instead of going to the last semester of high school. I was so distraught over Gene's death that I couldn't concentrate on studying, anyway. Took a couple of years to get back to it and study for the GED exam, but I did it. Perseverance. I'm well-stocked with that.

My roommate Jill wants to go to the grocers before Tammie gets home, so I have to run. Tomorrow is Tammie's birthday, and we want to bake her a cake.

CHAPTER TWELVE

OHN DASHED OFF an email with suggestions on how the presentation to the board should be improved. The board meeting was coming up and the directors on his team were frantically trying to align behind the messages to be shared.

He glanced at his watch and sighed. It was only three-thirty; he expected another four hours in the office before he could justify leaving for the day. Long days like this had been fine in his forties and fifties. And for the last few years, he hadn't minded them because staying busy helped keep the bouts of grief at bay.

Meeting the lovely florist had eased his sadness and loneliness; he hoped it was a permanent reprieve.

Thinking about Anna Lee, he called his assistant, Mary, to his office.

"Hi, John. What can I help with?" she asked, entering the room with a notepad and pen in hand.

"Would you do me a favor and order a dozen roses for me?"

"Roses? Who are they for?" she asked, raising an eyebrow.

"A lady I met. Order them from In Bloom and say that your boss will pick them up. Give them your name on the order, so she won't know it's me coming to pick them up. She works there, and I want to surprise her."

Mary smiled. "Absolutely. Will you pick them up tonight?" She glanced over at the clock on the wall.

"No, order them for pickup tomorrow afternoon. Say, four p.m. That will be a nice incentive to get out of here early tomorrow. It's going to be a late night tonight." Besides, he planned to take Anna Lee on a date Friday night, and the flowers would be a perfect touch.

"Sounds good. I'll call now."

She left and John reviewed his notes for the upcoming meeting.

Mary was back in five minutes. "Sorry to bug you, but In Bloom is closed."

"Closed? What do you mean?"

"There was a recorded message saying that because of unforeseen events, they would be closed until Saturday."

John felt a deep worry churn in his stomach. Was Anna Lee all right? Had she taken ill or gotten hurt?

He'd tried to call her yesterday, but she hadn't answered. What had happened?

"Until Saturday? Then they will reopen. That's got to be positive, right?" he asked.

"I think so?" She looked at him, concern apparent in her eyes and tight mouth. "Do you want me to drive by there and see if I can find out what's going on?"

He glanced at his watch. He had that meeting in ten minutes with his boss. "No. But call Carl and tell him I need to reschedule. Something urgent came up."

"Yes, of course." She spun on her heel.

He grabbed his laptop and shoved it in his bag without shutting it down, hoping it wouldn't overheat before he had the chance. Grabbing his car keys from the desk drawer, he left.

JOHN DROVE STRAIGHT to In Bloom. Arriving, he pulled into the parking lot and looked at the dark building. The building itself looked fine, but he noticed the flower planters and benches near the entrance.

"Strange," he muttered.

Thankful he knew where Anna Lee lived, he didn't stop but pulled out of the lot. Ten minutes later, he drew up to the curb in front of her house. The lights were on in the front window and in the upstairs turret room.

He bounded out of the car and up the sidewalk. Reaching the front door, he rang the bell and waited several minutes, shifting his weight from one foot to the other and whistling, trying to ease his mind.

Just when he was ready to pound on the door with his fist, it opened. Anna Lee stood in front of him wearing a purple tracksuit. It was the first time he'd seen her in something other than a dress.

"Anna Lee? Are you all right? I heard the store would be closed for a few days…"

"You did? How?" She seemed tired, and he worried that she'd gotten a fright or been hurt, though she didn't appear to be.

"My assistant called to order flowers, and she got a recording."

"Ah. Wait. Why are we standing in the doorway? Come in."

She bent over and picked up the cat before it could sneak out the front door. Moving aside, she pointed to a chair on the far wall.

He sat and watched her make her way to the couch. She put Salty down and gave his ear a rub before sitting next to him.

"A truck hit the building. One of the pillars out front. The engineer wanted it repaired, and I thought it best they do that work without customers going in and out. I'll reopen on Saturday. They'll be done by then."

"A truck? Oh no! Is insurance covering the damage?"

Anna Lee nodded and leaned back so the cat could crawl on her lap.

"Yours or the truck driver's?"

"He had good insurance, thank heavens. All in all, it will be fine. Gave Salty and me a little scare, but in the grand scheme of things, we got off pretty good."

"Were you there when it happened?"

"Yes. It was a supply delivery—they always come during the day—with a new driver. He just got too close."

"He wasn't hurt?"

Anna Lee smiled. "No, thank goodness. Not physically, anyway. His pride might have taken a bit of a bruise."

"I'm thankful you weren't hurt. Will the insurance cover your lost sales, what with having to close?"

"Not sure yet. Probably need to make another phone call tomorrow. I can't remember the last time I had to close for a couple of days. Hope I don't lose any customers because of it."

She yawned, and John leaned forward. "Are you sure you're OK?"

"I'm fine. But the commotion took a bit out of me. I'm grateful for the couple days of rest. Saturday will be a busy day. I have two weddings, so it will be hectic. I can go in tomorrow afternoon and do some prep work without opening the store. That will help. Saturday will be all hands on deck. All the girls will be in. Not sure Salty will go in, though; he was traumatized. He was lying in the front window, fast asleep, when it happened."

"Oh, poor kitty," John cooed. "Good thing you're both all right. I wanted to ask you out to dinner tomorrow. Would you be able to go if you have to go in and work?"

"Reckon I gotta eat. Dinner sounds nice. What time are you thinking?"

"Six?"

"That's all right. I'm looking forward to it. Can I get you something to drink now? Or eat? Are you hungry?"

"No, I won't impose. I should go now that I know you're OK. There's a big presentation my team is working on, and I rushed out of work early to come check on you."

"Going back to the office?"

"No, I can do what I need to do from home." He thought about the laptop in the car, hoping again it wasn't overheating. "I'll get out of your hair. You should rest. Please call me if you need anything."

He was sad that she hadn't called him either yesterday or today to tell him what had happened. Maybe someday he would be the first person she would think of when things happened in her day. He could hope.

CHAPTER THIRTEEN

June 1, 1988—I've got myself in a mess but good. I bought a run-down, abandoned old gas station in Bloomington that will someday, hopefully sooner rather than later, be my floral shop.

Benefit of buying something old and abandoned? It was CHEAP! Well, I still had to sign my life away to get the loan, but still was much cheaper than I expected it would be. I've driven by that place for a few years and was so intrigued by it. Felt like I was in an old black and white movie. I could picture the mechanics standing outside, smoking cigarettes with their greasy white t-shirts and denim pants.

Feeling blessed that Mrs. Carrington didn't get angry when I told her I was leaving to start my own floral shop. I was worried that she'd make me quit right away, afraid I would take business away from her. Be a competitor. A long time ago, she and Mr. C. had talked about opening a second location in either Washington or Bloomington, but when Mr. C. got sick, they stopped talking about it. I thought about approaching them to see if they would let me run their second location, but the more I thought about it, the more I realized I wanted to run my own business. Make all the decisions and accept responsibility for the mistakes myself. I know I can do it. I'm smart, capable, and creative. Willing to work hard.

I'll need that gumption. It's going to take some hard work to get it in shape, but it's only a mile from my apartment building. After work each night, I can stop there and work on it for a few hours before I go home.

Wish I had a bathtub in this apartment. It would be nice after a long day of work and an evening of cleaning, painting, and remodeling.

I have a clear vision of what I want. I'll make one of the garage bays into a large workroom with a giant table in the middle—lots of room to spread out supplies to work. Maybe someday I'll have a helper or two, will need room for that. The middle garage bay will become a place to see clients, show them portfolios of my work, write up orders, and even interview help. The main part of the building will be the retail space. I see lots of shelves for gifts and a large flower cart with grab-and-go bouquets. I'm even going to use the existing register and counter. The counter is the perfect height and length. It just needs refinishing, once the layers of disgusting green paint are scraped off. The register is ancient, maybe original to the building. It makes me smile just to look at the old buttons and the hand crank for totaling up.

I can't wait to get started. But tonight, I'm going to draw up the space and put my ideas on paper. A dumpster will be delivered on Monday, and I can start removing all the old junk. Can't wait!

<blockquote>I should see about getting into the beauty parlor and getting a new perm done first. Then I won't have to worry about fussing with my hair every day.</blockquote>

ANNA LEE WALKED John to the door and watched him leave. He'd leaned over and given her a light peck on the cheek before he left. The feel of his lips against her cheek warmed her heart. She didn't realize how much she wanted his presence until he'd shown up. That he rushed to her when he'd heard the store was closed was endearing. It had been so long since she'd had someone show up for her like that. The feeling that there was someone there to share her burdens and worries was foreign to her.

She closed the door behind him and turned off the porch light; she didn't want to encourage door-ringers this late at night.

Walking through the front room, she clicked off the two lamps. As she headed towards the kitchen, Salty hopped off the couch and followed her.

She hated to go to bed with dirty dishes in the sink. As she tidied the kitchen, she thought about John's visit and the look of concern in his eyes when she opened the door to him. He was a go-getter. He'd shown that quality in several ways already in the short time she'd known him, and she liked it. It was comforting to think that she might have someone to rely on after going at it alone all her life.

Staying home from the shop today gave her the opportunity to clean out her freezer, go through her spices, and wipe down the cabinets. A little spring cleaning. Keeping busy eased her mind.

The insurance agent had called earlier and said that further analysis had found no major issues, and once the pillar was reinforced, everything would be as good as new. Maybe not as good as when it was first built in 1925, but good.

That bit of news brought a smile to her face. She wouldn't lose a lot of business, closing for only two days. She'd brought her order book home and would go in on Friday to create the arrangements needed that day, without opening the store to customers. And Saturday she'd be back to business as usual.

After she washed the dishes and put them in the drainer to dry, she glanced about the room. Soon she would swap the winter curtains for light, gauzy summer ones. Honoring the change in seasons was important to her: it was a natural way of life that she appreciated. Times for growth, for rest, for rejuvenations, waxing and waning like the moon. Marking the months, seasons, years, and decades.

A honey pot on the table caught her eye. It was almost empty, so she put it on the counter next to the sink. She'd fill it in the morning.

April 26–My bones are tired and so am I. Why is it that staying at home and piddling around can be more exhausting than a full day at work? Salty might appreciate staying home on a Thursday, but I don't. Hope none of my customers were disappointed to come by and find the store closed today. Couldn't be helped. Good news–they say the damage was minor and the work will be done tomorrow.

John stopped by tonight. He was worried when he heard the store was closed and he rushed over here to check on me. Imagine that. It was nice to see him, didn't realize how down I was feeling. His visit cheered me up.

He asked me to have dinner tomorrow night. Almost like a courtship. Can't get too far ahead of myself.

I don't think I deserve someone like John. He's a good man with a good family. Old-fashioned values. Lost his poor wife. I can still see he's grieving, like recognizes like.

He wouldn't be interested in me if he knew my whole story. I couldn't keep my own child. He raised three. How could he love a woman that let her child slip out of her hands?

Dinner is fine. It's friendly and companionable. Have to remember my place. And that's here in this rambling old house. With my memories. With my heart safely guarded.

CHAPTER FOURTEEN

THE RESTAURANT'S LIGHTING was practically nonexistent. John had to use the light from his cell phone to read the menu. Once he'd decided on the filet mignon, he closed his menu and glanced around. The steakhouse's walls were a soft chocolate color, with touches of grainy wood and pictures of mountains dotting the walls.

He quickly turned his gaze back to his preferred view, Anna Lee. The sides of her hair were pulled back with hair combs, and she was wearing bright red reading glasses. She absently tapped her chin with a finger as she browsed the menu.

He liked the way she scrunched her nose when her glasses started to slide down.

She closed her menu and looked up at him, seeming surprised to see him staring. Soft pink color rose in her cheeks, her eyes twinkled, and she smiled at him.

"You're staring at me," she said, dipping her head and reaching for her water.

"I enjoy watching you. You're captivating."

"Oh, hogwash!" She waved her hand across her face. "You could charm the birds off the trees."

John laughed. Her funny sayings were a big part of her charm.

After the server took their orders, John asked Anna Lee about the progress on the repairs at In Bloom.

"They say it's ready," she responded, brushing her bangs out of her eyes. "Good thing, too. I've got a busy day tomorrow with weddings."

"What would have happened if it wasn't ready?"

"Well, my Plan B was to take all the supplies to my house and have the girls come over to create the arrangements there. You've seen my house—there's room, but not a good space for a bunch of women who need access to the same flowers and supplies. Would have used the dining-room table, and it would have worked, but it wouldn't have been easy."

She twisted her neck absently, and John imagined she was feeling the aches of the day ahead of her. She'd turned down the suggestion of wine, saying she needed a good night's sleep, and wine wouldn't give her that.

"It's good that you have a Plan B. We are always thinking about contingency plans with our work projects. The what-if and worst-case scenarios. It's good to be prepared for what might go wrong."

"I suppose. Didn't know I had 'a truck crashing into my building' on my bingo card for this year."

John laughed. "Right. I wouldn't, either. What emergencies do you prepare for?"

This wasn't the most romantic line of questioning, wasn't romantic at all, but it felt safe, and at least they were talking.

"Supply-chain issues. Having the right help. Sometimes the girls I hire up and quit because they got something better to do. Or they move without giving much warning. Though sometimes I don't think they give themselves much notice. Live for the moment, and all."

"Does that happen often?"

"Sporadically. I've got a wonderful group of girls right now. All of them have been with me a while, except Dominica. She's new. I like that young lady. She's clever, has got lots of ideas, and she likes to build things. Similar to me."

"You build things?"

The server brought their salads, and John reached for the salt and pepper shakers. He was liberal with the pepper but knew he needed to go easy on the salt.

"I rarely build things, but I repurpose them. Take broken things and turn them into something new. Hate to see so much set out for the trash. We're living in such a disposable time. Not good for the environment. You know, I remember my great-grandparents' place in Kentucky. They didn't have a garbage-pickup service. They had a small dump for things that absolutely couldn't be re-used, and they composted food waste for the garden. Containers of goods that they bought were often repurposed, making dresses out of flour sacks, for example."

She took a bite before continuing. "Did you know that back in the great depression, flour producers saw that women were making dresses and clothes out of flour sacks, so they started making them in pretty calico patterns?"

"No. I never heard that."

"They did. I think we need to get back to that—ensuring packaging can be recycled or repurposed. And don't get me started on fast fashion. Too much discarded clothing goes to massive landfills. I think there should be a two-year moratorium on all clothing manufacturing, except for some specific purposes—uniforms, wedding dresses, that sort of thing. There's plenty of clothes to go around if people would just look for alternative options. Open more thrift stores. Close all the brand-new clothing stores."

"Wow!" John chuckled. "You've got a strong opinion on this topic."

"I do, and I'm not going to apologize for it."

"You shouldn't. I like people with opinions, and I like a strong woman. I hope I've raised strong daughters."

"You have doubts?"

John lifted his glass of wine and watched as he swirled it around. "In lots of ways, I know they're strong. Like knowing and going after what they want. They're aces, all of them, but they're dealing with grief. Deana and Tara are still struggling. I think Kelley has it a little easier being a mom, in a way. She must be strong for her kids. And she says she can see a little of her mother in each of her kids; that gives her joy and peace. I'm sure she still gets sad and has moments of grief, but overall, she's OK. We can talk about Margaret and laugh about the good times, and we can talk about the terrible sickness and the pain she had at the end. But we can talk about it. With the other two, if the subject comes up, it's like I've poured gasoline on a lit stove. Whoosh! Instant combustion and flames. The flames being tears in this case. It's still too raw for them to talk about."

"How long did you say it's been?" Anna Lee reached across the table and put her hand on his free one.

"Five years." He swallowed a large gulp of the wine. It burned his throat, which helped keep the tears at bay. *Now look at this. I'm doing exactly what I complained about my girls doing.*

"There's no timeline for grief. If anyone tells you there is, run away. When we love someone deeply, we can go on, the pain and grief can ease, but it never truly goes away. You can hum along, think everything is fine, life is good, you're living again, and then you are in the grocery store, and you pick up a can of their favorite soup, and you're bawlin' in the aisle."

"Spoken from experience, I take it?"

"Something like that."

"You're right. It can sneak up on us and knock us down. And I'm not trying to rush my girls to heal, but it makes me worry about them. I guess that's what we do as parents, right?"

A look of pain crossed Anna Lee's face, and John wished he could take his words back. He didn't know where that pain came from, but he knew there was more to her story. He hoped one day she would trust him enough to open up and share.

"Right," she said. The server approached, and she looked up appreciatively when her dinner was placed in front of her. "This looks wonderful."

John agreed. He used the interruption to break their conversation thread. He cut into his steak to make sure it wasn't too pink and asked Anna Lee how long she'd been in her home.

"Thirty years. I love that old broad."

"The house?" he asked, laughing.

"Yep. Never named her, exactly, but she's a grand painted lady."

John knew ornate Victorian houses like Anna Lee's were called painted ladies. "She is. Don't you worry about all those stairs as you get older?"

"It's not as easy as it used to be to get up and down, I'll give you that," she agreed. "But I hope to die in that house. Hate the idea of going into a nursing home to while away my days. But, if it happens, it happens. Can't borrow trouble. What about you? What's your house like?"

He needed to invite her over to see his home soon. It would be weird having another woman in it, when Margaret had been the lady of the house for so long.

"Two-story, but thankfully the primary bedroom is on the first floor. It was great having the girls upstairs when they lived at home, close but not too close. Since Tara moved out, I hardly ever go up there. I have a cleaning lady who comes every other week, and she dusts and vacuums the upstairs. Yes, it's big, but it's great when I have the whole family home for the holidays."

Anna Lee leaned forward. "And you have memories of your wife there. That's a blessing."

John smiled ruefully. "A blessing and a curse. Though I don't know how my girls would react if I said I was selling it. That might hurt them too much."

"It's admirable that you care what they think, but I can't imagine they would be mad if you told them that you wanted a smaller house. Less to maintain."

"I hope you're right. No proper plans to move now, though, so I…" He paused, laughing. "Won't borrow that trouble today." He enjoyed using Anna Lee's turn of phrase.

"Good for you."

CHAPTER FIFTEEN

ANNA LEE FELT thrilled that this second date had gone as well as the first. It was fun getting to know someone new and hearing about his life with his late wife and daughters. She tried not to let any jealousy over his family life rear up and chew on her heart. At seventy, it was too late for her, and she had accepted that.

It was obvious John loved his family by the way his eyes lit up when he talked about them. It made him a good man in her eyes. There were times he reminded her of Gene, especially in the way he listened intently to her responses to his questions. And the man asked a lot of questions! She appreciated his curiosity.

They turned down dessert in the restaurant. John said he wanted soft-serve ice cream, so they drove to Carl's ice-cream shop for sundaes. It was still too chilly to eat outside; they sat in John's sedan to eat them.

Anna Lee took a bite of her caramel sundae, relishing the sweet and creamy flavors. "Why haven't you retired? You said you were planning to when your wife got sick, but you still haven't. Why not?"

She wondered if his wife's sickness had taken a financial toll. She imagined he had good insurance working for a large company, but cancer was expensive.

"To be honest, I'm afraid to retire. It would give me too much free time. Too much time for the grief to overwhelm me. Working helps give me something to do, keeps my mind occupied. Don't know what would happen if I stopped."

She nodded. "I can relate to that. Not from a grief perspective, but from loneliness. Working with the young ladies, talking to customers that come in, planning weddings with brides and grooms, keeps the loneliness at bay. If I ever retire, I'll have to get a couple more cats, I guess. Maybe a dog, too."

"Maybe we both need a few more friends," John replied. "To stay busy and ward off the grief and loneliness."

"Huh. You think it's that simple? More friends?"

"Couldn't hurt."

"You know, my neighbor talked about going to an adult day care. Imagine that. But she said they play cards and games, socialize. There are even fitness and mobility classes. She enjoys it. Said it gives her something to do to pass the days. Maybe when we retire, we can find something like that."

"Why wait until we retire?" John scraped his spoon along the edges, capturing the last of the strawberry sauce in his sundae. "We should look for things like that to do now. We have our evenings free."

"Oh, I don't like to go out much in the evenings. Especially in winter. I prefer to drive my scooter, and I don't like to drive it at night. Not as easy for people to see me. Too many drunks at night, too. Plus, my eyesight…" She trailed off. Growing old was not for the faint of heart.

"My eyesight's great! I can drive us. I think we each need to look for something fun we can try. A group playing cards. A class of some sort. Or even a lecture."

"Suppose we're not too old to learn some new tricks."

"Of course not. I think it would be great. We can spend time together and with others."

"I like the sound of that, John. It's a good idea. I used to play some cards as a kid. Maybe we could find someone to play rummy with, or euchre."

"I'll ask around and let you know what I find."

Anna Lee liked the way he took charge. She wasn't used to someone else leading; usually it was her or no one. Unless Tabitha reached out, wanting to get together, and then they took turns deciding when and where.

She finished her sundae and rested the empty cup on her leg. "This was a great night. You're easy to talk to. I appreciate that."

"You are as well. I'm enjoying getting to know you. You're spunky and pretty and fun."

Pretty? He called her pretty. She pushed her gray hair behind her shoulder. Running her hand down the side of her neck, she felt the slack skin and wrinkles. Seventy years took a toll on the skin. She tried not to curse the lines and wrinkles as they appeared. To her, they were badges of honor. It was a blessing to age—Gene and many others didn't get the chance. It was a dishonor to those that died young to lament your wrinkles, she figured.

"Thank you. You're an interesting man. I enjoy getting to know you, too."

John reached over and took her empty cup. He stepped out of the car and tossed the garbage in the trash can. "Ready to go?" he asked. "Do you need to stop anywhere on the way home? Groceries?"

"I'm ready, and no, I don't need anything while we're out. Appreciate the offer, though."

John started the car and put it in gear. "I know you have a busy day tomorrow, but can I see you on Sunday?"

"That would be nice. Not too early, though; I might sleep in."

"Sure. How about I pick you up at noon? Lunch and an afternoon matinee?"

Anna Lee laughed. "I haven't been to a theater in years. Sounds good."

"Me, either. Look at us striking out and doing something new already!"

WHEN THEY APPROACHED her house, Anna Lee asked John to pull into the driveway and let her out close to the back door. She didn't tell him she'd left the back door unlocked and didn't want to fool with the key for the front door.

He put the car in park and opened his door. "I'll come around," he said, before exiting the vehicle.

She waited for him to open her door. Such a lovely gesture.

"Thanks, John, for the wonderful evening. I feel spoiled. Next time, I will get the check."

"Nope. That's not how it works. I ask you out, I pay."

"Fine. Then Sunday, I'll remember to ask you out next."

John chuckled and put his hand on her lower back as she began walking towards the back stairs. When they reached the bottom of the stairs, she turned to him.

"Thank you again. I had a lovely evening."

He smiled, and the wrinkles around his eyes and mouth deepened. She wanted to reach up and touch his face, so she did. She placed her palm on his cheek and smiled back at him. He leaned forward and gently placed his lips on hers. She closed her eyes and returned the kiss. He took his time kissing her good night and they could have been there for seconds or hours. It was a blur to Anna Lee. A fluttering sensation swept over her body—butterflies in her stomach and goose flesh spread across her skin. All the sounds she had noticed a moment before–crickets, a car in the back alley, and a few birds settling in for the night–quieted and she heard her heart beat thrum in her ear.

When he finally stepped back, she felt herself blush and was thankful the glow from the streetlight didn't shine too brightly here.

"Good night, John," she said before placing a hand on the railing.

"Night, night, Anna Lee." He watched her climb the stairs.

On the back porch, she watched him walk to his car. Once he'd reached it, she opened the door into her kitchen.

She'd left a lamp turned on just outside the kitchen and the light from it illuminated Salty, who was sitting on the floor, looking at her with curiosity and maybe disdain.

"I fed you before I left you, silly cat," she said. With a sigh, she added, "Want a treat?"

The cat's tail thumped once, and he walked to his bowl. Anna Lee retrieved the treats from the canister on the counter.

She contemplated writing in her journal, but decided sleep was more important. It had been a rough week, and she would need her wits and extra energy for work on Saturday.

"I'll meet you in the bed, Salt," she said, locking the back door.

She plodded upstairs to the second floor, glancing once toward the back room. Maybe it would be easier to move her bedroom to the first floor. She'd still have to go to the second floor for her bath, though, so leaving the bedroom upstairs for the time being would be better. Maybe she could ask Trevor to expand the first-floor powder room into a full bath.

CHAPTER SIXTEEN

I T WASN'T UNUSUAL to have two weddings on a Saturday during May, June, and August, but it was a little unusual for April.

Paige, Lauren, and Tilly were sitting around the large worktable in the garage bay and talking about classes while they worked on boutonnières for the first wedding. Anna Lee bounced back and forth between the retail store and the workroom. These girls had been with her for a while, and she trusted that they needed minimal direction and supervision.

Ringing up a customer who wanted a lavish bouquet for a dinner party, Anna Lee daydreamed about when she would be retired. Perhaps on some Saturday in the future, she would plan her own dinner party and would run out to buy flowers. Would In Bloom still exist? Would she have sold it to someone, or would it close? Perhaps be an abandoned building again? She shivered, hating the thought of the doors closing for a long time. She'd worked hard to bring new life into this place. She'd seen the potential, and she'd made it happen.

Once the customer had left, she ambled back to the workroom, smiling to see Salty following her. He jumped up on the worktable and nosed his way under Paige's arm.

"Oh, Salty! I don't have time for you, cutie patootie!" Paige murmured as she pressed her lips to the top of his head.

"That durn cat," Anna Lee said, picking him up and putting him back on the floor. "Go mind your own business. We got work to do."

She walked around to see the number of completed items on the side table. "How's it going, ladies?" she asked.

"Good, Anna Lee," Lauren replied, taking charge as usual. "We're just about done with the first wedding."

Anna Lee glanced at her watch. "Wonderful. I'll call the delivery driver and tell him we're about ready for him."

"All righty! And remind me about the driver," Tilly said. "Is this the scrumptious one?"

Anna Lee shook her head. Tilly was always interested in cute boys. "You'll have to judge for yourself. What do I know about those things?"

"Well, is he our age, at least?" Tilly persisted.

"A little older, I reckon."

Tilly wiggled her shoulders. "I can't wait to meet him. It's nice to meet new people."

"You mean new men," Paige retorted. "Who's got time for that? Finals are coming up, and then I'm leaving for my internship."

"Right, there's more to college than meeting new men," Lauren added.

"Says you," Tilly volleyed.

Anna Lee loved listening to the good-natured banter between the young ladies. *This keeps me young. And not so lonely.*

The thought reminded her of the conversation with John about when to retire. What would she do if she didn't have this? She'd sit at home all day and spy on the neighbors. That wouldn't be terrible, but she didn't want to become captain of the neighborhood watch or anything.

Plus, she had weddings booked out until November of this year, with a few consultations on the books for weddings next spring. She was in demand. That counted for something. She wouldn't want to let down the brides who sought her out.

"Right, Anna Lee?" Lauren said.

"I'm sorry, dear, I didn't catch what you said. Must have been daydreaming," she replied.

"I was telling Tilly that you hired a new person for the summer, since Paige and I will be gone for a couple of months."

"Right. I think you'll like her; she's starting soon."

The room was warm from the abundant sunshine streaming through the glass in the bay door, and heady with the smell of roses. Anna Lee picked up the clipboard with the wedding details and fanned herself. "Whew. It's too warm. I'm going to raise the garage door a bit to get some air in here."

The girls called out "Sounds good" and "All right" and "Righto" (that was Tilly) as Anna Lee pressed the door opener and raised the door five feet. She trusted Salty to stay close if he had the gumption to wander out.

She stood and watched the traffic go by for a few minutes. A red pickup pulled into her lot and parked. Not too close to the building; the planters and benches were still in place.

She walked outside slowly and opened the front door for the customer who was approaching.

"Morning," she greeted the young man with acne scars.

"Hi," his voice cracked. Anna Lee wondered what he was looking for.

"Can I help you?" she asked him.

"Mom sent me in for a bouquet of tulips, if you have them," he replied.

"You're in luck. I do," she responded.

As she helped the kid pick out tulips, she thought about how they brought joy to people. They reminded her of Easter and new dresses for church, early spring and longer days. They were such lovely flowers to give to friends. She decided to send some to John at work.

She didn't think she deserved love; it was best not to think like that. But she deserved a new friend, and John was shaping up to be just that.

February 14, 1969–It happened! It finally happened! Gene kissed me! It was the most glorious, amazing, sweetest thing to ever happen to me!

After school, we walked to the park with his sister and her friend. Gene tried to teach us to play pinochle, but we were all clueless. I find it hard concentrating on cards or conversation when he's around. We tried to be good sports, but I could tell he was frustrated when we didn't catch on within ten minutes.

The other girls grew bored and left, which was groovy—Gene offered to walk me home.

After we crossed over Euclid Ave., we ducked into an alleyway behind the grocery store, and halfway down the alley, Gene pulled me into an opening between two garages and he kissed me!

I couldn't believe it! He'd taken my books and carried them under one arm. With the other arm, he twisted his fingers in my hair and studied it for a moment. I thought I'd faint before he leaned over and brushed his lips across my cheek. I had to turn my head fast to kiss his lips. I think I surprised him, but it didn't take him long to kiss me back.

My very first kiss. I have nothing to compare it to, but I know it was the best I'll ever have. It felt as if all my muscles turned to honey. They were instant liquid. I grabbed hold of the front of his jacket and pulled him closer to me. He laughed, which unfortunately broke the kiss.

We heard footsteps in the alley, so Gene pushed me out and told me to walk on. He waited and came out of our hiding spot a minute later. He caught up with me and I wanted to hold his hand as we walked home, but he said that wasn't a good idea.

Well, I'm not letting that spoil what was the BEST day of my life!

CHAPTER SEVENTEEN

"WHOA! WOULD YOU look at that!" Anna Lee gleefully pushed the button to recline the large leather seat at the movie theater. Once it stopped, she kept clicking forward and backward to find the perfect position. The movement almost made her dizzy.

She couldn't remember the last time she'd been in a theater, but she knew the seats hadn't reclined then. She could get used to this!

John chuckled as he eased his seat back. "I'll try not to fall asleep. Maybe we shouldn't have had lunch before the movie."

"I hope it's interesting, or we may both be snoring before long."

Anna Lee pulled the plastic bag of homemade chocolate chip and pecan cookies out of her purse. She'd baked a small batch that morning from her frozen dough. *Good thing I have a big pocketbook.*

She handed John one of the cookies and waited anxiously for his response. He rolled his eyes back and groaned. Anna Lee laughed at his antics.

Soon, the lights dimmed, and the previews started. John reached over and took her hand. She turned and smiled at him.

The feel of his hand was comforting and exciting. She did not want to let go! She leaned back in her seat with a pleased smile on her face.

Anna Lee thought maybe she should be bold and send John roses instead of tulips. That would put her heart on her sleeve. *No, too soon. I need to keep him in the "friend-zone"*, she chuckled to herself. She'd heard that term from Tilly. Those girls kept her hip.

Speaking of hips, hers was aching. She adjusted her seat back a little more. *There, that's better.*

During the drive back to Anna Lee's house, John suggested she meet his daughters. She'd asked if it was too soon—they'd only known each other for a couple of weeks. John disagreed; he felt it was time. He said his daughter in Chicago was teasing him, saying she thought he was making it up. He wanted to prove to his family that he wasn't.

Watch your heart, lady. Meeting his family would make this real. If she wasn't careful, she'd start making long-term plans, and there was no time for that. Not when she had a business to run, a large home to maintain, and a fat orange cat to serve.

He'd also told her about an important meeting with the board coming up on Tuesday morning. He said he felt he and his team were prepared, but she could tell he was a little nervous about it.

Anna Lee had nodded when he told her, knowing that Tuesday afternoon would be the perfect time to send flowers to him at work.

CHAPTER EIGHTEEN

TUESDAY AFTERNOON, JOHN ordered in lunch for his team to celebrate the successful board meeting. They crowded around a large conference table, recapping everything that had gone well and discussing ways that it could have been better.

John smiled as he looked around. This team had grown in the last couple of years. He watched Malcolm lead the discussion and thought it was time to turn over even more responsibility. He would talk to his boss about his retirement transition plan; he knew Malcolm was ready to take over his position.

It would be good to promote from within, and John felt pleased with his effort to coach and mentor Malcolm and the others who reported to him directly. But it was almost time to step aside and turn his attention elsewhere. To himself, his home, his daughters, and to Anna Lee, if she'd let him.

Mary knocked on the door and walked in. "Sorry to interrupt. But I knew you were all in here celebrating and these arrived. I thought they'd make a great addition to the table."

She carried a large vase filled with at least two dozen yellow tulips.

"Did Barton send them?" John asked. Barton was the president of the company and had congratulated John on the team's performance at the board meeting earlier. It wasn't like Barton to send flowers to the team, but it was a special meeting.

"I don't think so," Mary said hesitantly. "But I didn't open the card. It's addressed to you, John."

He pulled the small card from the center of the bouquet. The cover had a tiny "In Bloom" logo in the corner, and his name was in fancy script in the middle. *At least they came from Anna Lee's shop.*

It wasn't his birthday, and it wasn't any special date having to do with Margaret that he could think of; he didn't think they were from his daughters.

He pulled out the card as the room quieted. *Am I supposed to read it aloud?*

He didn't. He scanned it quickly before sliding the card in his pocket. It read, "John, sending these to celebrate your big meeting. I know it went well. Can't imagine you'd do anything poorly. I planned to send the flowers before I even knew about your meeting. It's been a genuine pleasure getting to know you. Yours in friendship, Anna Lee Foster."

Yours in friendship? What did she mean by that? That she didn't want their relationship progressing any further? He thought it was going well! Not too fast, not too slow. They were still getting to know each other, but he felt they were extremely compatible. His forehead tightened, and he rubbed it, trying to loosen the tension.

"Everything all right, John?" Malcolm asked from the front of the room.

"Yes." John looked up and scanned the room. They were looking at him with concern on their faces. He smiled to reassure them. "They're from a friend. Congratulating us on a great board meeting."

It was mostly the truth. The smiles he received back were exhilarating. He quickly tempered his emotions. If he didn't watch himself, he'd give everyone the afternoon off.

He wanted the afternoon off so he could go see Anna Lee and try to decipher the full meaning behind the message. Had he been moving too quickly for her? He could slow things down if she wanted, but he wanted to keep moving forward and not regress.

It had been forty years since he'd dated Margaret and he had to admit the times had changed. Maybe he needed advice from someone other than his oldest daughter. He glanced around the room. Most of the people on his team were in their thirties and forties. None of them had experienced divorce or the loss of a spouse.

He had let some of his friendships fade to the background when Margaret got sick. His best friend Evan still tried to keep in contact, but things hadn't been the same between them. As he dealt with his grief, he had a hard time talking to his friends who still had their wives.

He sighed. Maybe it was time to call up Evan and suggest they get together. He knew if he was going to contemplate retirement someday soon, he would need friends.

Malcolm asked if John had any further questions or suggestions for the team. If not, he thought they could adjourn the meeting. John agreed and dismissed everyone. He gathered his notebook and the vase of yellow tulips and made his way back to his office.

Mary came to his office as soon as he put the flowers on his desk. "Who are the flowers from?" she asked.

"The owner of In Bloom herself."

"Oh!" Mary's eyes widened in surprise. "That's wonderful. Funny how you were concerned about her last week, and now she's sending you flowers."

"It is funny how life works sometimes. Hey, do I have any more meetings this afternoon?"

"Just a one-on-one with Malcolm at three."

"Can you move that? I would like to take the rest of the afternoon off."

"Sure. Are you going to leave the flowers here or take them home with you? They are beautiful."

John nodded and smiled. "I'll leave them. They brighten up the space."

"They do."

ANNA LEE WALKED the young bride and her mother to the front door. They had finished a wedding consultation, and Anna Lee was pleased with the discussion and even more pleased with the booking for August.

As the mother and daughter exited, Anna Lee glanced at her watch. Still an hour to go before closing. As the door opened, a warm breeze entered the space, and Anna Lee could smell the scents of spring—the sun warming the grass that was coming back to life and the earthy smell of the dirt in the planters outside the door.

She walked outside and picked a few dead leaves off the plants in front. She looked at the repaired pillar and was thankful that the repair was complete. Since there was no one in the store and nothing urgent to do, she sat on one of the new benches. Plopping on the bench, she closed her eyes and lifted her face to the sun. The warmth on her face was comforting, like God was telling her everything was going to be fine.

The sound of a car coming closer filled her ears. Must be a customer. Since she'd not gotten to pull an April Fool's joke on anyone, she thought she'd just sit peacefully, pretend to be asleep.

She heard a car door open and close, but she continued to sit motionlessly. Footsteps grew louder. She wondered if this person would talk first or shake her to make sure she wasn't dead.

They did neither. She felt someone sit down beside her on the bench. She remained motionless.

"Beautiful afternoon," the man said. She recognized John's voice.

Keeping her eyes closed, she let out a little breath of air. "It is that."

"Good, you're not asleep."

"No. Just enjoying a moment of meditation."

"That's wonderful. I'll sit here quietly, too."

And he did. It pleased Anna Lee that he didn't need to keep making small talk or just noise. It was comforting to know that he was there without demanding her attention. *This is what a real relationship feels like.*

After a few minutes of rest and sun, she opened her eyes and blinked a few times. She glanced over at John, and he was sitting as she had been—head tilted back and eyes closed. He had a slight five o'clock shadow, and he was wearing black slacks with a white dress shirt and a red tie. She loved the bold red tie.

"Hi, there," she whispered, not wanting to startle him.

He kept his eyes closed for another moment and smiled. "Hi, yourself. This was a treat." He opened his eyes and turned towards her. "I stopped by to say thank you for the flowers. That was a special gesture."

"I'm glad you liked them. I hope it didn't embarrass you. How'd your meeting go?"

"Fantastic. The team performed magnificently, and we got everything we asked for."

"That's wonderful. Glad to hear it. Guess they let you out early today." She glanced at her watch; it wasn't even three.

"I took some time off." He glanced towards the road and cleared his throat. "I wanted to thank you for the flowers…"

"You said that."

"And…I wanted to ask about the message. You said, "yours in friendship."

"I did. We're friends."

"Yes. I agree. But I wanted to see if the door was open for more. I like you a lot, Anna Lee. I love spending time with you and getting to know you, and I think there's a real chance of this becoming something special. I want to make sure I'm not alone in those feelings, that I'm reading the room, so to speak."

"Ah. I see."

She looked down at her hands. She kept her fingernails short and filed, but she didn't see the need for polish. Since she used her hands frequently in the flower shop and garden, they would constantly get chipped if she applied polish. They were working hands. And aging hands. She rubbed her thumb over the lines on her right hand, the blue veins easy to see through her pale, thin skin.

She assumed John's late wife probably had regular manicures, being the wife of a business executive. She probably led the life of a "lady who lunched" and served on charity boards, fighting for good causes, and sitting on the PTA board to ensure her kids' education was supported. Anna Lee admired the moms who got involved and made good things happen.

John was here, asking for more than friendship. He was a good man. She wanted to stop being a wallflower and try a relationship. But she was afraid she didn't deserve it. He was a family man, and she'd let her tiny family, her own daughter, slip through her fingers. Once he knew that, would he look at her the same way? She feared he'd run. She should tell him soon, but not today.

She looked up at him with a smile. "I didn't want to be too forward and suppose it was more than friendship, but if you're willing to give it a chance to blossom into more, I am."

He reached over and took hold of her hand, rubbing the back of it with his thumb, as she'd done. He smiled. "I'm pleased to hear that. Do you have any plans for dinner?"

"No. What do you have in mind?"

"Tacos!"

He said it with such enthusiasm, Anna Lee laughed. "I'll have to take Salty home first."

"I'll pick you up at six."

He said he needed to run home to change and gave her a sweet kiss before leaving. She made her way back into the shop and gave the cat a few back rubs as she passed him lying in the window. "Salty, looks like we're going to try this relationship thing. Get used to seeing more of John around."

The cat opened one eye and yawned, arching his shoulders, and sticking his front legs out in a big stretch. After stretching, he pulled one paw up onto his nose and went back to sleep. *He must not have a problem with John. Maybe he'll like the extra attention.*

June 18, 1969–Today was Gene's birthday, and I gave him a beautiful leather wallet with his initials on it. He said he loved it. He surprised me with a gift, too. I told him he shouldn't do that. It's his special day. But he insisted. It's a pretty silver bracelet with a small heart charm. I love it and will always wear it.

I thought today was perfect, but then he had to go and ruin it. He told me he's decided to sign up for the Army. He thinks the discipline and training he gets there will serve him better than getting a job, and he can't see any way to pay for college or vocational training.

He wants to marry me when I graduate next year but worries he can't afford to support me and a family without better prospects.

I'm trying to be supportive, but I'm so scared. There is a war going on, and I'd rather he wash dishes for tiny wages than risk going into the service. I said that too, but he told me not to worry, that he promised to come home to me.

That's going to have to do. I tried to tell my mom how I feel about Gene, but she wouldn't listen. She told me it's just a crush and that it'll pass. She's wrong though. This is LOVE!!!

CHAPTER NINETEEN

THE FOLLOWING SUNDAY, John turned the blinker on and braced himself for Anna Lee's reaction to his home. Would she like it? Would she be comfortable?

He'd asked her over on the pretense of getting her ideas on how to improve his landscaping, but he didn't tell her he hoped that one day she'd live there with him, and he thought it would be nice if she put her mark on the yard. He hired a well-known landscaping firm, and he had an appointment with them to talk about changes, but he wanted her input first.

"Well, here we are," he said, as the car turned into the long driveway.

His home was in the Tanglewood subdivision, which had been developed in the early eighties. It was an executive home community with one-acre plots and stately homes. It had been perfect when they'd bought it, before the girls were born. They were planning for a family and felt pleased when they were blessed with three children. Their five-bedroom home accommodated all of them comfortably.

Memories of Margaret and the girls filled the home. All the Christmas and birthday parties. The summer swimming parties in the large, in-ground pool in the backyard. Teaching each of the girls to ride a bike in the driveway, running after them as they wobbled and righted.

He watched Anna Lee from the corner of his eye. Her head was moving side to side and her eyes were taking it all in.

"Whelp," she said. "It's beautiful and tasteful, with lots of mature trees. I can't wait to see the flower beds."

John parked and turned towards her. "I can't wait to show you around."

"Let's get to it," Anna Lee said, raising her arm and pointing her finger, in a "lead the way" gesture.

John took her around the house, pointing at the evergreen bushes that lined the front walk and the daylilies that clustered here and there.

"Everything looks so neat and orderly. You must work hard maintaining this large yard," Anna Lee said.

John put his hand on her lower back and guided her around the side of the house, where landscape lighting dotted the shrubs. "I don't have a green thumb like you. I hire a great landscaping team."

"I'll tell you what." Anna Lee raised a finger and shook it at him. "I'm envious of all the perfectly placed mulch. My yard needs mulch, but I am dreading the backbreaking effort."

"I'd be happy to send my team over there to take care of that for you," John replied.

"Naw." Anna Lee shook her head vigorously. "I'll do it. My yard is not as big as yours. I don't need a lot. I can do it perfectly well. Just takes me a little longer than it used to. Like most things."

In the backyard, he pointed to the row of rose bushes just past the swimming pool.

"I imagine it's a lovely place to sit when they're blooming," Anna Lee said. She pointed to the screened-in gazebo where the family had loved to gather in the evening, away from the mosquitoes and other bugs.

"It is. We spent many evenings in there playing games, enjoying the fresh air." He paused and watched her take it in. "Are you hungry? Why don't we go in? I'll start dinner, and we can talk about your thoughts on how to improve the yard. If you like, maybe you could meet the landscaper with me next Saturday."

"I'm hungry. But I can't meet next Saturday; we have a full day at In Bloom, with a large wedding."

"Right. I keep forgetting about your Saturdays."

Margaret had rarely worked during their marriage; she'd focused on raising the girls. Once they had grown and started moving out, she'd taken a few jobs here and there. John wasn't used to having to consider someone else's commitments when he made plans.

"I'm busy most Saturdays with weddings from April through September. It's one of those things. I love that I have Mondays off, though. I can go out shopping and run errands when things are a little quieter than on the weekend."

John led the way to the back door, which he could unlock with a digital thumb print. "That would be convenient. Let me give you a tour of the house, then we'll settle in the kitchen."

He led her from room to room, trying to see it through her eyes. Yes, it was big for a single man, but each room held cherished family memories. The formal living was where they would place their Christmas tree, and John would be filled with joy as he pulled into the driveway each evening, to see the large bay window filled with twinkling lights.

School pictures of the girls lined the walls in the more casual family room off the kitchen. It was a joy to see each of the girls go from four years old to eighteen in a matter of seconds as his eyes scanned the walls. He and Margaret had talked about taking them down and redecorating once, but neither could bring themselves to do it.

Upstairs, the girls' bedrooms were now guest bedrooms, more for the girls when they returned home than for other guests. Margaret had redecorated each one when they had left, though she kept a few key things from each girl in the rooms. In Kelley's room, the bookcase was filled with some of Kelley's favorite stories. John often thought about emptying it and taking the children's stories to Kelley for her children to enjoy, but he hadn't yet.

In Deana's room, two of her American Girl dolls remained, standing watch on the dresser.

And in Tara's room, one of her old skateboards hung on the wall. He still shook his head, thinking about the little tomboy she'd been until she turned seventeen, and a beautiful swan emerged.

Anna Lee made observant and respectful comments during the tour. John's heart swelled, pleased that Anna Lee didn't seem intimidated or uncomfortable in his home. He thought if things continued to progress, maybe someday she'd be comfortable joining him here.

Since the primary bedroom in his home was on the main floor, it would be easier for them in future years than climbing an extensive set of stairs at her house. It was the more practical of the two options if their relationship progressed that far.

John shook his head. How difficult would it be to have another woman live in the house he'd shared with Margaret for so many years? Would the memories of Margaret take precedence, or would he be able to create a new life for Anna Lee here?

He'd never considered the question before he met Anna Lee. It had seemed a moot point, so there was no reason to mull it over. But now that he was showing Anna Lee the home and imagining her here with him, it was time to consider it.

His head might have questions, but his heart did not. He would manage—and manage just fine. He could blend history with new opportunity.

"That's the house. Let's head back to the kitchen," John said as they left Tara's bedroom.

"It's a beautiful home, John." Anna Lee said, following him down the stairs, holding onto the railing. "I can see your wife's touches throughout. And I can almost hear little girls running up and down the stairs, or a gaggle of kids splashing in the pool. The house obviously saw lots of love and holds lots of memories."

John turned and beamed when he reached the first floor. "It does. I'm glad you see that."

Anna Lee followed him to the kitchen, where she asked if she could do anything to help prepare their meal.

"No. It's under control. I'll get the grill going. Have a seat and relax. Can I get you something to drink?"

ANNA LEE SAT at the large round kitchen table with six padded chairs around it. The chairs were on coasters and easy to move. "No, I'm fine for now."

"Good. Back in a flash."

John walked out the back door, and Anna Lee's eyes swept the room, going over everything with a more patient eye. This was the heart of the home, and it showed. There were several snapshots of John's two grandchildren on the refrigerator. John's briefcase and a pile of mail sat on an open roll-top desk against the far wall. Anna Lee could imagine John's wife sitting there, planning meals for the week, putting a grocery list together, paying bills, jotting important school dates for the girls on the calendar. All those things that a loving, happy wife would do.

It was obvious that his wife's passing had left a lasting mark on John. He seemed interested in her, but Anna Lee felt like a consolation prize. Maybe that's just how you felt when you met a widower in your seventies.

For the next twenty minutes, John bustled in and out, whistling Beatles tunes and making small talk. Anna Lee watched him and marveled at how gentle and kind he was. She felt blessed to have met him, and she hoped they would grow even closer. But she wondered if the memories that surrounded him here would allow his heart to open to her fully. Would he be capable of loving again? She wasn't sure. She reminded herself to guard her own heart, lest it be trampled on like dead leaves in the fall.

Growing restless, she walked to the family room and studied the pictures of John's beautiful daughters lining the wall. It was a little disorienting to watch them grow twelve years in a matter of seconds. She clasped her hands together, nervously rubbing one finger as she made her way back to the kitchen.

Once the steaks were ready, they ate and talked about their plans for the week. John brought up the idea of having dinner with his two daughters who lived in Bloomington, and they agreed to try for Saturday evening.

Anna Lee hoped it wasn't too soon to meet them. She worried she would care for them too much, too fast. And if their relationship didn't work out, she might find her heart broken over John and his daughters.

September 13, 1969–I received a letter from Gene today. Luckily, I got the mail first. If mom had seen it first, I don't know if I ever would have.

He said he's finished all his training and will deploy to Vietnam soon. He's not sure he'll be able to write to me for a while.

I'm just crushed and so worried–can't eat–I've lost five pounds since he left for basic training. I'll waste away to nothing before he gets home. Can't concentrate on schoolwork; I am falling behind and worried about my grades. Not sure what to do. My parents are threatening to set me up with someone to "snap me out of my funk". But I don't want to see anyone else. Mom keeps telling me I'll be upset if I miss the formal dances this year. I don't care about the silly dances.

I'd like to get a job to fill the time, but Mom says not until I can prove my grades aren't suffering, so that won't happen.

CHAPTER TWENTY

JOHN PICKED HER up and drove to the restaurant where they would meet his daughters, Deana and Tara, for dinner.

Anna Lee took extra time getting ready, even applying makeup, which she didn't normally do. She was dressed in a crisp linen pant suit in deep purple with a soft pink flowery blouse. She wore small silver hoop earrings and a silver chain with a small butterfly around her neck.

John made the introductions in the restaurant lobby. Deana had John's blue-green eyes and the same shy smile as her dad. Anna Lee thought Tara must have taken her looks more from her mom; she was blond with large, round blue eyes.

At their table, Deana asked about Anna Lee's business. Deana was engaged to be married the following year, so she was curious about different wedding flowers. She showed Anna Lee a few inspirational photos she'd saved on Pinterest.

Anna Lee felt confident and excited about how the conversation was going with Deana. Talking about flowers always put her at ease.

Looking over at Tara, who'd been quiet for most of the evening, Anna Lee wondered what she could say to break the ice with the young lady. She'd answered direct questions but hadn't contributed to the conversation.

"Tara," Anna Lee said, "your dad told me you're the one who took him to the steampunk festival. What did you think about it? Was this your first time going?"

Tara put her fork down and put her hands in her lap. "I thought it was interesting. Lots of cool costumes. And yes, it was my first time. That's where you two met, huh?"

John leaned forward. "Yes! Anna Lee was selling flower crowns and other interesting items. I bought a top hat." He smiled at Anna Lee. "I guess you could say you're responsible for our meeting."

Tara rolled her eyes. "Don't remind me."

Anna Lee sucked in a breath. *How rude!* She had to hold her tongue. As offended as she was, she would not have words with John's daughter the first time she met her.

"Tara," John said in a low voice. "Apologize."

"I'm sorry. I didn't mean it. I'm just having a day."

Knowing that everyone has off days, Anna Lee smiled. She would not let one remark sway her opinion of John's daughter.

Tara picked up her fork and stabbed at a piece of her steak. "So, Anna Lee, have you ever been married? Have any kids? Dad hasn't shared much."

Wow. This kid came out with heavy questions.

"Tara!" John chided. "You don't have to answer those questions," he said to Anna Lee.

"No, it's all right. Never married. No kids."

"Oh, never been in love," Tara assumed.

"I didn't say that. I've been in love. Sometimes life doesn't work out like we plan it." Needing to change the trajectory of this conversation, Anna Lee asked a question of her own. "What do you do, Tara?"

"I'm a buyer for Harrington's Department Store. I specialize in home products. Linens, soft goods, some decor."

"Wow. That's fascinating. Do you get to travel for work?"

"Yes," she said, her eyes lighting up. "I attend several trade conferences each year. That's the best part of the job, traveling from coast to coast. I hope to travel internationally next year, but I need to get a promotion first."

"Well, I hope you get that promotion soon, and you get to go." Anna Lee asked Deana about her job as well, and the conversation seemed to flow a little better from there.

When John dropped her off at home, he parked in the drive and held her hand as he walked her to the back porch.

Once they reached the steps, Anna Lee turned to him and kissed him on the cheek. "Thank you for a lovely evening. It was wonderful getting to meet your daughters."

He raised an eyebrow at her. "Are you certain about that? I wish Tara had been a little better-behaved. Not her best showing."

"She's not a horse, John. Everyone has bad days. She's not ready for you to date; she's still grieving for her mother. Margaret must have been a wonderful mom."

Anna Lee did not miss the tears that sprang to John's eyes. She reached out and clutched his forearm. "You've done a great job raising your girls. I hope I get to meet Kelley some time."

John pulled her into a hug and stood, embracing her quietly. After several seconds, he gave an extra squeeze and released her. "You are a good woman. Thank you for your understanding. I'll work on getting Kelley and her family down here to meet you." He leaned in and kissed her softly, his lips warming hers. "I'll call you tomorrow."

"Good night, John."

Anna Lee let herself in as John walked back to his car. Inside the house, she tossed her pocketbook on the kitchen table and sat down, pulling off the dress shoes that, it turned out, were a little too tight on her. She dropped them on the floor.

Glancing at the clock on the stove, she decided to take a hot bath. She needed one after the evening with Tara. Anna Lee knew an antagonist when she saw one.

January 18, 1970–My hand is shaking, and I can barely see the paper in front of me. I can't write the words. I can't. My mind is racing with questions that have no answers. What am I going to do now? How will I raise this baby on my own? What kind of job can I get without graduating?

It's like the baby knows what's happened and is grieving too. The baby has been so active. Normally I feel him or her shift and kick or just roll around in there, as happy and as playful as a young kitten. But ever since Gene's sister called me and told me the horrible news hours ago, I haven't felt the baby stir once.

I don't know what to do.

And my heart won't stop tearing itself in two. I feel it ripping and disintegrating one tiny thread at a time.

CHAPTER TWENTY-ONE

JOHN CALLED ANNA Lee early on Sunday and apologized again for his daughter's behavior.

"It's fine, John. Give her time," Anna Lee had said.

He appreciated her words, but he was worried when she declined his offer to get breakfast or lunch together. She said she had to paint some birdhouses she sold in the flower shop, and that she'd be busy all day doing it.

He'd seen those birdhouses in her shop, but he wasn't sure if that was the full story. He worried that Tara's hostility was pushing Anna Lee away.

He wanted to storm over to Tara's apartment and have a word with her but thought it best to wait until his temper cooled. Talking to Kelley would cheer him up, so he called her instead.

"Hi, Dad! How did the dinner go last night?" Kelley inquired as soon as she answered. One of her sisters must have told her about the plans.

"It went."

"That doesn't sound good."

"It would have been fine if Tara hadn't been a brat."

Brat was the best word he could think of to say.

"Oh, no. I hope she didn't scare Anna Lee off."

He rubbed his hand over his face. "Hard to say. I called Anna Lee to ask her to breakfast or lunch today, and she said she's too busy. On Sunday!"

"People can be busy on Sundays, Dad."

"I know that." John fiddled with a pen and notepad sitting in front of him. "But I'm worried it's something else. I don't have a good feeling about it."

"I can tell by your voice. Well, maybe send her flowers to get on her good side?"

"Kells, she owns a florist shop. I don't think that will impress her. Oh, she sent me flowers last week."

"She did? What kind?"

"Tulips. Yellow tulips."

"Oh, that's adorable!" Kelley gushed. "You're right, though. Sending her flowers probably won't work. How about sending a singing telegram? A big gesture."

"Singing telegram? Seriously? Seems a little goofy, even for an old man like me. I'll think about it." Not wanting to dwell on how worried he was about the situation with Anna Lee, he changed the subject. "Hey, I miss you and the kids. It's been too long."

"I know. Busy couple of months. Do you think you could come next Sunday? Spend the day with us? You could even drive up on Saturday night and stay the night. The kids would love to see Papa."

"That sounds wonderful. I'll plan on it."

"Great! Looking forward to it!"

And he was. He needed some time with his grandkids. They always put joy in his heart.

A COUPLE OF hours later, John gritted his teeth and dialed Tara. He wanted to lay into her as soon as she answered, but he decided to take a more laid-back approach.

"Hi, Dad." She sounded normal, like she hadn't ruined dinner the previous evening. "How are you?"

"Not great. I'm still seething over your behavior last night." So much for the kinder, gentler approach he'd planned on.

"Ugh. I apologized to her last night. What more do you want?"

"I want you to act like the twenty-seven-year-old woman that you are. I've never seen you be so rude to someone before. What were you thinking?" He patted himself on the back for not shouting.

"I don't know. I…I feel like she's hiding something."

"Are you nuts? Hiding something? Anna Lee is one of the most honest, straight-forward people I've met in years. She's kind, warm, generous. I don't think this has anything to do with her as a person. I think it's more about you."

"Think what you want," Tara replied, "but I think she's just after you for your money. She's probably a gold digger. Never married? At her age? In her generation? Something's fishy."

"Tara Lynn Peerson," he said through a clenched jaw. "The only reason I'm not tearing into you is because I think you're not ready for me to date. You're uncomfortable with the idea. But honey, it's been five years since your mother passed. And I'm going to date. And if you didn't ruin my chances with Anna Lee, I'm going to continue dating her."

John heard Tara take in a breath, but she didn't respond for several seconds. He was determined to wait her out.

"Fine," she finally spoke. "I still don't like it. I think there's something up, and I feel I need to point it out. I love you, and I don't want to see you hurt."

John chuckled softly. "I appreciate you looking out for me, but I got this. Remember, getting hurt is a risk we take when we search for love and happiness. It's a risk I'm willing to take. The potential returns are worth the risk. And it's better than being a lonely old fart, wandering around the rooms of this big house alone."

Tara gasped. "You wouldn't sell the house, would you? It's not too big! It's perfect for family gatherings. Like for Christmas. We can all be home for the holidays."

"I said nothing about selling the house. Maybe someday there will be someone here to share it with. For the other 364 days of the year."

He knew he was getting ahead of himself. They'd only been on a handful of dates. It was too early to think about which house they might live in if they were married.

But what if they married? Would Anna Lee want to move into his home? Or would she want to stay in her home? She'd said that she'd been there a long time and planned to leave on a stretcher.

At some point, they might need to think about combining assets, estate planning, and wills.

"Dad?" Tara's voice interrupted his thoughts.

"I'm sorry, kiddo. My mind wandered off. What were you saying?"

"Nothing important. I need to run. I'm meeting some friends for brunch. I'll see you soon?"

"Yes, let's try to get together later this week. Oh, I'm going to Kelley's on Saturday and staying until Sunday, so how about Thursday?"

"OK, Dad. Sounds good to me."

She hung up and John jotted a few notes on the pad of paper.

1. Make apt. with financial adviser

2. Call Deana

3. Find will

4. Follow up with landscaper

Since he had the day to himself, he decided to organize his financial papers, think about his financial future, retirement, and his will. With or without a significant other.

CHAPTER TWENTY-TWO

ANNA LEE REMINDED her heart to be cautious. John's daughters didn't seem ready to share their dad with someone else.

She hadn't seen John since last Saturday. Though he called during the week, she declined each of his suggestions to stop by or grab a bite, needing time to build the walls back up around her heart. She knew that if this relationship had any chance of growing stronger, she had to tell him about giving up her baby for adoption. John might not want to see her again, and she worried the heartache would be too much to bear. But she had to come clean. He had a right to know who she was, to know everything, good and bad, about her. If they were going to move forward, she needed to get this secret off her chest.

On Friday, she finally relented and agreed to go to dinner. During the meal, they caught up on the highlights of their work-weeks. When John mentioned he was considering retirement, Anna Lee shared that she'd been thinking more and more about it herself, though no final decisions or dates were in place for either of them.

John shared some ideas about getting her business appraised as a piece of information that would probably help her decide. He suggested starting with her accountant, and if that didn't work out, he'd help her research other options.

"There is one other thing I wanted to throw out," John began. "You're going to think I'm crazy for bringing it up now. And I hope it doesn't frighten you off. But I have strong feelings for you, and I can see a future together."

Anna Lee pushed the bite of chicken she was about to eat around on her plate. She waited for him to continue.

"As I told you, I've been thinking a lot about retirement and the next phase of my life. I've been going over financial numbers and thinking about some major life decisions. Like—" he paused and took a breath. "If we stayed together and maybe, perhaps, got married at some point, where would we live?" He chuckled softly. "My house or yours, is what I'm trying to get at."

Anna Lee dropped her fork and leaned back in the chair. "Whoa. We could count the number of dates we've had on one hand, I think. That seems a little sudden."

"Right. Right. I know." He ran his hand over his salt and pepper hair. "I'm a planner. I'm always thinking ten steps ahead. Some of that is my job. Some of it is just my personal quirk. I was worried it would scare you off. Forget I brought it up."

Anna Lee leaned forward and smiled. "You couldn't scare me off. But I think we still have some getting to know each other to do before we make big decisions like that. Don't you?"

He nodded.

"I love my home, John. It's like my second skin. I couldn't imagine leaving it willingly. But let's not get too far ahead of ourselves."

John looked disappointed, but Anna Lee felt strongly about this. She'd seen his home, and it carried too many memories of his late wife. She didn't want to be a third wheel in her own home. Maybe they could be companions and stay in their own homes. It wasn't unheard of.

After the server cleared their dinner plates, they ordered coffees and some carrot cake to share. Anna Lee steeled herself for the confession she still needed to make.

"John, there is something that I think you should know about me. I'm not saying this just because you are talking about what home we would live in if we were married. I planned to tell you this before you picked me up tonight."

She paused and searched John's eyes. He still seemed open and trusting. She expected that would change when she finished.

"On our first date," she continued, "I told you about falling in love with Gene as a teenager and that he went off to war and didn't come home."

John nodded and reached out to take her hand in support.

"What I didn't tell you is that I'd gotten pregnant before he left."

She observed him carefully and noticed the intake of breath.

"I didn't think you had children," he finally said. "Did you…" he couldn't finish his question.

She dropped her head, no longer able to maintain eye contact with him. Her voice wavered as she continued. "Without the support of my family, without the possibility of college, without a spouse, I did the only thing that I thought would make it right. I gave my baby up for adoption."

The words nearly choked her. It had been nearly fifty years since she'd shared this story with anyone. After sharing with a couple of close friends and seeing how they judged her, she'd stopped sharing. It was easier to keep it bundled up inside.

She waited for John to respond. She raised her eyes to look at his thumb, which was stroking her hand. It was comforting. He hadn't pulled away when she'd dropped her bombshell.

"I can't imagine the pain that caused you," he said after several moments. "You are a strong woman to have made that decision. But I'm surprised you didn't fall in love again later and marry."

She looked up to see if he meant what he said. His eyes were solemn, filled with the same sadness she felt. How could she have found a man who would understand? Who would accept this truth and not judge her too harshly?

"In some ways, I think it was a self-imposed punishment. How could I allow myself to fall in love again, possibly get married and have other children, when I gave up my first? A child that I loved and still love with all my heart. I thought I was doing the right thing, giving her to a family that could provide for her. Could love her. But I don't know, maybe it was selfish of me and not selfless."

John spoke gently. "Sometimes we decide with the best information we have at the time. I think you did that. You can't keep punishing yourself for a decision you made at eighteen."

Anna Lee sat in silence, thinking about what he'd said. Her mind told her he was right, but her heart said otherwise. "There. That's my deep, dark secret. If you don't want to see me again, I'll understand. It must be unfathomable to someone who married and was lucky enough to have three children."

"Not unfathomable," he responded, as he continued to hold her hand, running his thumb over it. "I understand, from a different perspective. We wanted kids right away, but we had trouble conceiving. It took three years for Margaret to get pregnant. We had been talking about adoption when we got the news that we were going to be parents. It was the greatest feeling in the world. But in our initial research into adoption, we often discussed the heartache it must cause a woman to carry a child for nine months, then give them to someone else to raise. It's the ultimate gift. I'm sure whoever raised your daughter felt that blessing."

"I hope so. I don't know if anyone ever told her she was adopted. No one ever knocked on my door, telling me they were my child. So, if she was told, she wasn't interested in finding me. That's her right."

Anna Lee sat back in her chair, pulling her hand away from John. "That's my story. Thank you for listening. It feels good to share it. Sometimes hiding that secret makes me feel like a shadow of myself. People may be close to me, and they may know me pretty well, but they never know all of me."

John leaned forward. "Thank you for sharing that with me. I know it was hard to do. For the record, *I* want to know all of you."

When the waiter came with the cake, Anna Lee waved it away. She couldn't eat it now. John asked for the cake to be boxed up to go. Seemed he'd lost his appetite after her confession, too.

ANNA LEE WAS thankful to be at work on Saturday morning. She needed to stay busy to keep her mind off John.

He'd dropped her at home after dinner and said he was going to Chicago to visit his daughter and grandchildren today. While she wanted to be happy for him, she felt that he was already pulling away from her. He sounded colder and more distant. And he hadn't walked her to her door.

She knew telling him about Anita Gene, the name she'd given her baby, was the right thing to do, but it still hurt that he'd distanced himself. Though he said he understood, as a man with three daughters whom he loved, she was sure he couldn't really understand.

On top of her worries about John, today was the day that Lauren was leaving for Europe. Over the years, she'd told herself she was a fool for hiring young college girls who would move on after a year, or four years, if she was lucky. It always caused her heartache when they left. But she enjoyed the life and laughter they brought.

Lauren would be back before school started in the fall, she reminded herself.

As Anna Lee finished putting money in the register, Paige walked in from the back door, carrying a tote bag and a coffee mug. "Morning, Anna Lee!"

"Mornin', Paige. How are you?"

"I'm OK." She tossed her tote in the office and came up to the register, setting her coffee down and tying on an "In Bloom" apron. "I'm bummed that Lauren's leaving today. Makes me even sadder that I'm not going to New York for my internship this summer." There had been a mix-up, and her summer internship had fallen through.

"I am, too." Anna Lee hugged Paige tightly.

"Aw. I needed this," Paige said, hugging back. "You give the best hugs!"

Anna Lee chuckled. "You don't know how much I needed that hug."

"What's wrong?" Paige asked, stepping back and studying Anna Lee's face.

"Ahh, nothing to be concerned about." Anna Lee patted Paige's forearm. "Why don't we get busy and forget our troubles?"

"If you say so. But I'm a good listener if you need someone."

"I know you are, dear. I'm all right." She picked up the order book. "Let's look at what we have today."

Being busy would help push John to the back of her mind. She couldn't forget him completely, but she could get through this workday without breaking down in tears. That was good enough for her.

February 10, 1970–It's been almost a month since I learned Gene won't be coming home. A lot has changed.

I've moved into a maternity home in Peoria. I have a sweet roommate, Betsy. She's from Palmyra, IL which is southwest of Springfield. I had to ask, as I've never heard of it.

My baby will arrive sometime next month. I'm no longer counting down the months and weeks. If it were possible, I'd keep the baby inside for always.

It's been made perfectly clear to me that I can't afford to raise this baby on my own. Gene's parents won't help, my parents won't help. The Army won't help because we weren't married.

I attend group therapy meetings here. It's helpful to not feel so alone. We're all struggling with the decisions before us and talking about it helps sometimes.

On a happier note, I've learned to knit and I'm making a bright yellow dress for the baby to go home in. I know it's a girl, but just in case, I'm also making a white and blue blanket. I'll give the blanket to another girl when my baby leaves in the yellow dress.

If I have time, I'll make a dozen blankets for other babies. What else am I going to do to pass the time?

CHAPTER TWENTY-THREE

JOHN USED THE nearly three-hour drive to Kelley's house to mull over his dinner with Anna Lee. He beat himself up for bringing up the idea of combining houses. It was too soon. She was right; they didn't know everything about each other yet, and here he was, ready to talk about marriage.

Maybe Tara was right, and he wasn't using enough logic in this relationship. There was no way he was going to tell Tara that Anna Lee *had* withheld something, and something important, from him.

He didn't fault her. That wasn't the sort of thing you brought up to someone early in a relationship. Why would you bring that up with someone if you thought things wouldn't work out?

There was some comfort because she'd shared the news when she did. He had talked about a long-term relationship, and she'd wanted him to know this important piece of information.

But the matter of the house was weighing on him. His girls would be upset if he sold the home they'd grown up in, the home that housed so many memories of their mother. How could he take that away from them? How could he take that away from himself?

Anna Lee was being too stubborn, insisting she'd remain in her house. A hundred-year-old Victorian was not the house for someone in their eighties or nineties. He was amazed that, in her seventies, she still climbed up and down those stairs every day. It made him appreciate his first-floor bedroom all the more.

When he finally arrived at Kelley's, he was surprised to find Deana and Tara there as well. They all went out to a fun, kid-oriented place for dinner and laughs. The adults stayed up late playing board games and talking.

On Sunday morning, John woke up feeling both content and sad. It was fun to be all together under one roof, but he woke up missing Anna Lee. He wished they were at a point in their relationship when she would have come with him. She still hadn't met Kelley or his grandkids, and he thought she'd enjoy getting to know them.

He made his way to the kitchen and found Kelley there alone, nursing a cup of coffee. "Mind if I join you?" he asked.

"I've been waiting for you," Kelley said. "Thought about waking you up. It's like our Sunday morning phone call, but in person."

"Right." John fixed a coffee and sat across from her at the round oak table.

She pushed a box of banana nut muffins toward him. "The other girls being here last night surprised you, right?"

"It did. A wonderful surprise."

"Good. I was worried Tara would blab and ruin the surprise."

"She didn't." He thought about Tara ruining dinner with Anna Lee but held his tongue.

"How are things going with your lady friend? Did you see her this week?"

John thought about the secret that Anna Lee had shared. Not something he would share with his girls, and not something he wanted to dwell on. He thought about his mistake of talking about consolidating houses too soon. Maybe Kelley *could* give her old man some good advice.

"Well, not great. She seems to have put up some walls after the dinner with the girls. Holding me at a distance. And then we went to dinner Friday night, and I might have scared her off by talking about long-term planning."

"Oh? Like what?"

"Which house we might consolidate to."

"That seems a little soon, Dad. I can understand her hesitancy."

"I'm afraid I've pushed her away. She seems set on staying in her house and didn't seem at all interested in moving into mine."

Kelley nodded. After a pause, she said, "Can you blame her? That house is Mom's place. I think it would be hard for any woman to move in there with you, Dad."

"But how could I leave that house? It's where you girls grew up. It holds many wonderful memories." He thought about Tara's wish to keep having holidays there.

"Yes, it does." She stood up and refilled her coffee cup. "But the memories don't *live* in that house. They live in our minds and our hearts. We keep them with us."

"Hm, you're right. But I don't think we'll convince Tara of that."

Just as he said her name, Tara entered the kitchen. She still had on her pajamas and was rubbing her face. "Convince me of what?" she asked, stumbling towards the coffee pot.

John looked down at his coffee cup. This would not be easy. "Kelley and I were talking about how the memories of Mom are always with us. They're not held in the house."

"Sure—" Tara filled a coffee mug and looked in the refrigerator for cream. "You can't walk in and grab a memory off the book-shelf, but when I'm in the house, I remember much more. And I feel her presence in the house when I'm there."

"I know what you're saying. I do, too, Tara." Kelley watched her sister sit down next to her and reached over to squeeze her hand. "But I think it's important to keep in mind that if Dad sells the house in the future, it'll be all right. That's his right, and if he does, we need to support him."

John looked at Kelley. He hadn't said he'd sell the house. He didn't even say he was considering it. But she seemed to know that he needed this permission from his daughters. That it would be OK if he moved on—they would support his happiness and not hold grudges.

It felt as if everything in the house had quieted. The furnace had stopped blowing, the coffee pot stopped its hum. Everything seemed to hold its breath, just like him, waiting for Tara to speak.

She idly stirred her coffee cup. She sighed and pulled the spoon out, laying it on the table. "I don't know why you all seem interested in my opinion. It's not like I have a say in this."

John glanced at Kelley. That wasn't a yes or a no. Now what?

Kelley took the lead. "True. We really don't. But I think Dad wants to know that we'll support him, whatever he decides."

Tara looked at him and finally gave a half-smile. "I'm sorry I've been a pain. I am having a tough time letting go." Tears filled her eyes.

John raised his arms to her, and she crawled into his lap like a three-year-old. "It's not letting go. It's learning to live with the change. We all miss your mom terribly, but she wouldn't want us keeping our lives on hold to show we miss her. She knows we miss her."

Tara's shoulders shook slightly, and John continued to rub her back. Kelley's daughter, Maggie, waddled into the kitchen, dragging a small blanket behind her. She crawled into her mom's lap and looked at her aunt.

"Aunt Tata sad," she said, unable to pronounce her r's fully.

Tara laughed and sat up, wiping her eyes. "I am, Maggie. But I'm better now that you're up. What are we going to do today?"

Tara went back to her own seat and took a sip of coffee.

John blinked back his own tears. He suddenly felt as though he'd turned a corner with Tara. She was going to be fine.

"Now, Dad," Kelley said, shifting her daughter to a better position. "What are you going to do about Anna Lee? I think you need to go after her. Show her how much she means to you."

"I'm going to do just that. Wait and see."

CHAPTER TWENTY-FOUR

OHN TRIED CALLING Anna Lee before he left Chicago. He planned to stop at her house before going home, and he wanted to tell her he was coming. When she didn't answer, it didn't deter him.

As he drove, he mulled over Kelley's suggestion for a grand gesture. A flower bouquet from another florist was out. A singing telegram sounded ridiculous.

He replayed all their conversations in his mind, searching for something that would be meaningful to Anna Lee. Something that would prove to her that he listened to what she said and valued her thoughts, opinions, and views.

Since Anna Lee lived alone, he tried to think of an act of service. He wasn't sure that was her love language, but she didn't seem to put a lot of value on shiny new gifts, considering her point of view about too much stuff ending up in a landfill.

He didn't think sweet words would please her either, as she was a "shoot from the hip" kind of person.

He couldn't remember the other love languages, which was just as well. As he'd mulled them over, he knew an act of service was just the right thing. And it suddenly occurred to him what would be perfect. He hoped he had some ibuprofen in the car, because he was going to need it before the afternoon was over.

JOHN STOPPED AT a large nursery and got what he needed. He drove home to change into suitable clothes and headed over to Anna Lee's.

She wasn't home when he knocked. He glanced into the small garage where she kept her scooter and didn't see it there, so he knew she was out. Just as well. He wanted to complete this task while she was gone.

Ninety minutes later, he was finishing up when he heard the wheels of her scooter on the brick driveway. He was glad he'd moved his car to the curb before she got home, so he wasn't blocking her drive.

He was sitting on the back stairs, drinking a bottle of water that he had brought with him, when she stopped and pushed the kickstand down with the heel of her boot. She wore her usual long dress, tied into a knot just over her ankles, probably to keep it from flying up while she rode the scooter.

She dismounted and pulled her helmet off. He noticed a large baguette sticking out of her backpack; she must have been to the store.

She hung the helmet on the scooter's handlebar and turned to him. "John? What're you doing here? I thought that was your car out front."

He stood and smiled as she approached. "Hello. I was doing a little yard work."

"What?" Her eyes flew around the backyard. "You mulched!"

"I did. You said you were going to hire a kid to do it, and I decided I'd take care of it for you."

"But why?"

"It needed to be done, and I hoped it would make up for my arrogant assumptions about our future. I wasn't considering what you wanted, which made it seem like I was a bossy jerk, and I wanted to show you, by mulching, that I listen to you."

She shook her head, and John worried it hadn't been enough. If she threw him off her property now, he'd be devastated.

"You're full of surprises, John Peerson. I bet you're hungry after mulching. Want to come in for dinner?"

His shoulders released their tension. "I'd love that."

"What's that?" Anna Lee pointed to the bunch of flowers wrapped in newspaper that John had sprinkled with a little water to keep them from drying out.

"More wildflowers. I went back to the place where I found the original ones and picked another bouquet. I didn't want them drying out, so I poured some water in the newspaper pouch. That kept them looking pretty, I hope."

"It did. Bring them inside. I'll heat up some bean soup, and we can have a little chat."

March 18, 1970–My heart is breaking. They wouldn't even let me hold her. She was born on the 16th at 5:33 p.m. Though no one asked me, I named her Anita Gene. She has Gene's eyes and the shape of his chin. She has the most darling eyelashes, they're so long and so fine. She was nearly bald, and I wanted to scrub off the few hairs on her head so new growth would be nice and full. I remember my grandma saying that helped babies' hair grow.

I couldn't hold her, but I was able to touch her. Using my hands, I memorized every inch of her little head. I rubbed my thumb across her brow, over her nose and along the outer edge of her tiny baby ears.

She woke up and squirmed. I stroked the back of her hand and put my finger down where she could touch it. She grasped my finger and calmed down instantly. I nearly fainted when the nurse pulled her away from me. I was still lying in bed and too weak to get up and follow when they left the room.

I'm so sick. I can barely get out of bed to go to the bathroom. I just want to sleep, sleep, and sleep some more.

I asked Betsy to sneak to the nursery and take a couple of pictures of her on my camera. Then I'll always have the pictures. Betsy said she got a picture of Anita Gene wearing the dress I knitted for her. It's the dress she had on when—

Mrs. Lindstrom told me that the adoptive parents are very sweet and overjoyed. They've been trying to have a baby for four years with no luck. They live near Chicago, and he has a good job, though Mrs. L wouldn't tell me what he does.

Mrs. L wanted me to go to group therapy today, but I refused to leave my room. I sat by the window all day, hoping to get a peek of a baby in a yellow dress leaving. Betsy snuck a banana and toast in for me after breakfast, but I couldn't eat it. My stomach just roils at the thought of food.

I feel like such a failure. I hope Anita Gene never finds me. How could I look in her eyes and tell her I failed to find a way to raise her myself? She'll probably grow up thinking I'm the worst person in the world. How could a mother not fight for her baby? I was prepared to fight the bigotry, to work hard to make ends meet, to raise our baby up in a loving, supportive home. But that's when I thought I'd have Gene here to help me. Together, we would have been unstoppable, and our baby would have had every opportunity to do what she wants to do. I hope the couple who took her gives her that and more.

I hope one day this building is torn down. I've walked the halls at night, and I can hear the screams and cries of women and girls long gone. The building remembers the pain and presses it down on all the new arrivals.

I swear I'll never marry or have another baby. I don't deserve that kind of happiness after I let the best blessing of my life go.

CHAPTER TWENTY-FIVE

ANNA LEE LED the way into the house, placing her
backpack on the bench, and unloaded the groceries.
She'd taken her time shopping today, as it prevented
her from wandering around her empty house, feeling sorry for
herself, thinking about how things had ended with John.

Now that he was here, she wanted to pinch herself. It felt
like they were in a small canoe, struggling to keep from tipping
over and drowning. Having John show up to mulch her flower
beds without being asked made it seem like the canoe had hit a
sandbar—they were steady for the moment. She would wait and
see if they would stay upright or if the waves would carry them
out to sea again.

John asked if he could help, and she told him to sit and relax,
as he'd worked hard mulching. She got him a glass of iced tea
before she pulled the container of soup out of the refrigerator.

He sipped the tea. "I stayed with my daughter Kelley last night.
My other two girls came up, too, and we all stayed the night.
That was great. We had not all been together since Christmas."

"That's nice," she said, putting a pan on the stove and filling
it with soup.

"It was," John nodded. "We got a few things cleared up. Tara
finally came around to the idea of me dating again. Not that I

needed her permission, but having her acceptance takes a load off my mind."

"I'm glad to hear it." Anna Lee was tempering her reaction; she wasn't sure exactly where his mind was.

"The long drive was good for me. Lots of time to think."

"Yeah?" she asked. "What did you think about?" She gave the soup a stir, poured herself a glass of tea, and joined him at the table.

"You, mostly. And I thought about our future. I know I was too forward, thinking we might move into my house someday. I was thinking more about myself and my family when I said that, and not thinking about your wants and needs. I apologize for doing that. I should have asked you what you thought before assuming. You have a beautiful home here; I can see why you'd want to stay."

"It was my dream home when I bought it. I know you're looking at things from a practical perspective. And I've thought about aging in place a great deal. If it becomes too difficult to climb the stairs, I can turn the back sitting room into a bedroom. The first-floor doorways are all large enough for a wheelchair; I've measured them. I could get a wheelchair lift for the front steps; I know people who've done that. It could work. And like I said before, if I can no longer live alone and need nursing care, I'll go."

Anna Lee picked at the corner of a placemat. "You may think I'm stubborn about the house. But I must tell you that there's a little voice inside me that says I'll find my daughter someday, and she'll come to this house. That may sound goofy to you, but it's something I feel in my bones. I won't give up this house until that happens, unless I have no choice."

She sighed. She felt like she was giving John several reasons to run away. He could keep his solo canoe afloat and paddle away quickly.

"Oh, Anna Lee. That's a powerful reason to stay. I respect that. I won't ask you to leave."

She stood, walked to the stove, and stirred the soup. "I appreciate that. But aren't we getting ahead of ourselves? There are many things for us to consider about being in a serious relationship long term. Our careers, your family. It's complicated to marry at our age."

"Agree. And there are things we can do to mitigate them."

"Wills and prenups."

"Precisely."

"Seems strange to talk about a prenup at seventy, but it is the smart thing to do. Wait. How did we jump ahead to marriage? I think we should talk about our fourth or fifth date before we talk about marriage. There's no need to rush."

"Well, on one hand, that's true. But when you consider our ages, what are we waiting for?"

"How about I at least meet your other daughter and you meet my cousin Tabitha before we talk about prenuptial agreements or wedding bells?"

"You're on. So, are we in a good place, then? You see a long-term future with me, don't you, Anna Lee?"

Anna Lee turned off the burner. The soup was hot enough, and she walked back to John. He opened his arms to her, and she plopped down on his lap and hugged him in return.

"Yeah, John. I do." She kissed his cheek.

She did see that future. A future with John meant companionship, joy, caring, and love. It may have taken her fifty years after losing Gene to find love again, but she knew good things happened to those who endured.

April 8, 1992–First spring in my home and I have lots of plans to get this yard in shape. When I moved in last fall, I cleared out a lot of the brush and burned it all in an enormous pile by the alleyway. This spring, I'm finding lots of new growth and I want to see if it's friend or foe before deciding to keep, move, or remove.

The very first project I'm tackling is a flower bed behind the garage. I'm planting pink carnations and white lilies in a heart-shaped bed. I've seen a lovely concrete bench at the garden center that I'll place at the foot of the heart so I can sit and gaze upon it. They also have a three-foot-tall angel statue that I'll place in the middle of the heart.

This will be my memory garden dedicated to Anita Gene. When I sit out there and look at it, I'll say a brief prayer of remembrance and hope. A prayer to say that I remember her and that I hope we'll find each other someday here on earth.

Once the memory garden is in place, I'll make my way around the back, sides, and front. Not necessarily in that order. I will eliminate as much grass as I can and have flowers and plants that benefit the bees, butterflies, insects, and birds. Maybe I'll even put in a water feature. A bird bath near the back door for sure—that way I can bring fresh water out and fill it frequently.

There was a time when I thought I would never afford a home of my own, being single and all. But I finally did it! She's all mine and I'm just as proud as I can be. Call me a peacock and admire my feathers!

CHAPTER TWENTY-SIX

*L*IKE THE SUMMER days growing longer and warmer, her relationship with John followed suit. They fell into a comfortable rhythm, spending Sundays together, either at her house or his. They would make breakfast, read the paper, go for a long, lazy walk, do a few chores, go out to lunch, run errands, take a nap in the comfort of whichever living room they were in, and finally make dinner together. Each step became more and more in tune, and they could waltz around each other's kitchens in rhythmic movement, cutting, dicing, mixing, and sautéing.

In July, John took her to Chicago, where they stayed with Kelley and her family. Kelley's children took to Anna Lee immediately and she to them. They spent a day exploring at Brookfield Zoo, and Anna Lee wasn't sure who had more fun, she or the kids.

Getting to know John's daughters and being with them for several birthday parties began to give her the sense of family that she'd long desired. She wondered why she hadn't let down the wall around her heart a long time ago. She would have made a great stepmom in her younger years. At her age now, she felt like she could just be a 'good' one.

In mid-August, she was at In Bloom, working with her newest employee, Mack, when she got a phone call that nearly knocked her off her feet. It was a woman who said Anna Lee's daughter was looking for her.

The woman asked if it would be all right if she gave the daughter Anna Lee's phone number and address.

"Of course! There's no time to lose!" Anna Lee declared. She hung up the phone, scooped Salty up and dumped him unceremoniously into the backpack, grabbed her scooter keys, and left the store in a hurry. She had to get home, and now!

At home, she left the scooter in the driveway and rushed inside. She gave the cat some food not wanting him underfoot and hoping he'd soon trot off to a corner to sleep. She called John's cell phone and left him an urgent message to come over as soon as he could. She needed his support.

She was in the back room, searching drawers for the small box containing her few pictures of Gene and their baby, the bracelet that Gene had given her, and the blue and white baby blanket she'd made in case she'd had a boy.

Thirty minutes later, she heard a loud knock on her back door. Assuming it was John, she made her way to the kitchen. She felt as though she was walking through molasses, her feet moved so slowly. Glancing out the window, she was shocked to see Tilly at her door, but ushered her in.

"Tilly, come in. Come in." Anna Lee pointed to the table. "Have a seat. I'm surprised to see you here. Did something happen to Mack? Did she send you?"

"No, she didn't."

"Well, how'd you know I'd be home?"

Tilly raised her shoulders in a slight shrug. "Mack told me you left in a hurry."

"Oh, sure. Let me put some tea on. Do you need help with something? I must tell you, it's not the best time. I've got a lot going on. I've had some surprising news, and am expecting some company, but I would be happy to help you until they come."

Taking a seat at the dinette, Tilly clasped her hands and put them on the tabletop, leaning forward. "I know what your news is," she said softly.

Anna Lee's head spun. She couldn't process all this information at once. *Was I putting the teakettle on or getting water?*

"You do? How could you possibly know? Did Mackenzie overhear my conversation?" That was the only logical explanation. Until an hour ago, she herself hadn't even heard the news.

Tilly said the words Anna Lee never expected to hear come out of her mouth. "My mom, Irena, has been searching for her birth mom."

Anna Lee's hands flew to her mouth. How could this be happening to her? *Is this a dream? I must be dreaming.* She felt the tears flowing down her cheeks. "No," she whispered. "It can't be."

Tilly explained about finding the birth certificate and seeing Anna Lee's name on it. Tilly said she knew right away that it must be her boss, but her mom had cautioned against moving too quickly, advising her to wait until the information was confirmed.

The molasses seemed to have flowed into Anna Lee's mind. If what Tilly was saying was true, then that meant Tilly was…

"Then, you're—you're—" She couldn't get the words out.

Tilly smiled through her tears. "I'm your granddaughter. Yes."

"Oh, Heavenly Father!" Anna Lee looked up. "Thank you, thank you."

The teakettle whistled, and they both jumped. Tilly leaped up to turn it off, and Anna Lee sat on the bench. "Your mother is coming over tonight, right?"

Tilly confirmed and told Anna Lee that she'd wanted to be the one to break the news, since they already had a relationship. Anna Lee shook her head. *This explains the strange connection I've always felt with Tilly.*

If Tilly had been raised by her daughter, then her daughter must have been raised right. Tilly had obviously been raised with love and respect; those qualities were part of the core of her character. She had the easy way about her that came from someone who was secure.

Anna Lee said another prayer of thanks. After fifty years, she would finally meet her daughter and she had a granddaughter, whom she already knew! It was unfathomable.

"Tilly, do you have any siblings?"

"Yes." The girl smiled; her eyes sparkling. "A brother, Michael. He'll be here with my mom and dad."

"Two grandchildren," Anna Lee whispered. Just like John had, but much older.

JOHN ARRIVED A few minutes later, and Anna Lee filled him in on the news. He wrapped his arms around her and held her. Anna Lee relished the strength that his presence provided. She put her head on his chest and closed her eyes.

"Um, I'll go to the front room and give you two some privacy," Tilly said.

"Thanks, dear," Anna Lee said, never opening her eyes.

After a few minutes, she pulled back and looked into John's caring eyes, shocked to see the hint of moisture in them. "Can you believe it?" she asked.

"It's a miracle," he responded. "I know how much this means to you. I'm here to support you, and I feel very thankful that I get to be a part of your reunion with your daughter. Thank you for calling me."

She couldn't imagine going through this without him. Knowing how much he loved and cared for his daughters gave her strength. The next few hours might be hard. As much as she cherished the chance to meet her daughter, she knew Irena might raise some hard questions, and some powerful emotions might surface. She braced herself for the challenge.

"John, I'm trying to find a box of mementos and a few pictures. I want to show them to Anita— I mean Irena— when she gets here. Can you help me?"

"Certainly."

Together, they found the box quickly and took the baby pictures of Irena to the front room, where Anna Lee showed them to Tilly. They were exclaiming and sighing over the pictures when the doorbell rang.

Anna Lee took a sharp breath. This was it. She hurried to the front door and flung it open.

The woman standing in front of her took Anna Lee's breath away. She felt sure she would have recognized her as her own, just passing her on the street. She could see a resemblance to both her and Gene in the woman's features.

As soon as Irena smiled, Anna Lee leaped forward and hugged her. Stepping back, she held onto her daughter's arms as each of them looked the other up and down.

"You are beautiful," Anna Lee said, reaching up to stroke Irena's cheek. "You have your father's eyes and his chin. Still. I saw the resemblance when you were born."

Tears sprang to Irena's eyes, and she didn't brush them away as they slid down her face. "You're answering some of my questions already. May we come in?"

"Yes! Yes! Of course!"

As they entered the home, the men introduced themselves. When Michael introduced himself, it occurred to Anna Lee that Tilly's full name was Matilda. "Are you two twins?" she asked.

Everyone laughed. "No, they're two years apart. We just liked the matching initials," Irena said.

Anna Lee pulled Michael into a tight hug. "It's very nice to meet you."

He laughed and hugged her right back. "Likewise. Since Tilly's worked at the flower shop, she's shared stories about you, and

I feel like we have an advantage in getting to know you, but it's amazing to get to meet you in person."

"Yes, I feel the same."

She introduced them to John and asked everyone to settle in. She hoped they would stay for hours; there were fifty years to catch up on!

She insisted on sitting next to Irena, holding her hand. It was so incredible to finally have this moment to sit beside her daughter and hold her hand. She wanted to make up for all fifty lost years immediately.

If I died right now, I'd die in peace. She felt her face flush and reached for a magazine on the coffee table to fan herself.

"Are you all right?" Irena asked hesitantly.

"I'm fine. Fine. It's the excitement. My heart is still racing."

"Mine, too!" Irena laughed and leaned towards Anna Lee, rubbing her shoulder against her mother's.

"Don't mind me if I pinch myself," Anna Lee said. "It still doesn't feel real. When I got that call today—gosh, it was less than two hours ago! I felt like I'd won the lottery. I had always dreamed that you might try to find me, but after this long, I assumed you probably didn't know you were adopted."

"I've known for a long time, but I was torn about searching. I have wonderful parents, a happy life. I guess I thought it best to leave well enough alone. It wasn't until doctors discovered a spot on my mammogram that I thought it best to try to find out my birth family's health history. That scare led me on the journey to find you."

"And the spot?" Anna Lee asked hesitantly. She couldn't bear the thought that her daughter was ill.

"Fine. Nothing. A harmless mass."

"Thank the Lord!" Anna Lee exclaimed. "And what about your parents? Are they still alive?"

Irena nodded. "They are."

"Good. How do they feel about you searching for me?"

"They're very supportive. I told my mom I would call her later this evening, after we met you."

"That's wonderful!" Anna Lee took a quick breath before asking, "I would love the opportunity to meet them sometime, if they, and you, would be all right with that."

Irena's eyes lit up. "I'll make it happen."

Anna Lee wanted to pinch herself repeatedly. She looked into Irena's brown eyes and was whisked back in time to the day Irena was born, her wide, long-lashed eyes gazing at Anna Lee. She had whispered to the baby that she would never forget her, and she never had.

CHAPTER TWENTY-SEVEN

ANNA LEE GREETED Tilly, Michael and Ronin at the door, taking the container of cookies from Tilly and placing it on the dinette before giving her a quick hug. She couldn't get over the feeling of hugging her grandchildren. It was like Christmas morning every time.

"Come in! So good to see all of you! Glad you could make it," she said as the youngsters entered. John went to Chicago today to see Kelley and her family. While Anna Lee was a little sad he wasn't around, she enjoyed the chance to see her grandkids and Ronin alone.

"Thanks for inviting us, Grandma!" Michael said, pulling her into a big bear hug. At six feet tall, he towered over her.

She laughed as she pulled away, patting him on the chest. "You are such a great hugger. And it's great to see you again, Ronin."

Ronin gave her a quick hug as well. "Thank you for the invite, Anna Lee. We've been talking about this lunch for days. Michael cannot get enough of your home cooking."

"Well, I'm happy to cook for someone other than myself and the cat. Come in. Make yourself at home. You know the rules: there are no rules. But if you look bored, I'll put you to work."

She crossed to the stove and stirred the beef stew that had been simmering all morning. "I hope y'all are hungry. I cooked three pounds of beef. Yes, Michael," she said, smirking at him. "There will be to-go containers, before you ask."

"Yes!" He pumped a fist in the air.

Tilly was petting Salty, who'd jumped up on the bench next to her. "Grannie Annie, what can we help with today? Any special projects, now that you got these two fit and strong men here to help?"

The kids always offered to help her out, and Anna Lee kept a running list of little odds and ends projects she could use help with. She'd prefer to spend the whole time listening to them tell her about themselves, but she knew they got joy out of helping. They were raised well by their parents, always offering help and making frequent phone calls to check in.

"As a matter of fact, I do. But you all look like you're dressed for church. You can't do my dirty work dressed like that!"

"Grannie Annie, we all have a change of clothes in the car. We came prepared," Tilly responded. "Are we eating in here or in the dining room?"

"Dining room. It's all set. We just have to plate up and head in. The bread will be done in two minutes and we can eat."

"Yes!" Michael gave another fist pump.

"Grow up, Eminem," Ronin teased.

"Not gonna happen. Never."

"This is why you can't keep a girlfriend, bruh," Tilly said. "You refuse to grow up. You're like Peter Pan."

"Don't throw shade at Peter Pan like that," Ronin retorted. "He's way better than your brother."

Everyone laughed and Anna Lee smiled at the joyous noise. This was what her big old Victorian home should sound like; full of laughter and people. For far too long, it had felt more like a museum than a home. This year brought Anna Lee so many wonderful changes—meeting John, meeting Irena and Michael, discovering that Tilly, whom she already loved, was her granddaughter, and finally planning for retirement. She felt thrilled and at peace in a way she had never had before.

"All right. Let's eat. Plate up."

They moved on to the dining room, where they talked about their previous week's activity. Anna Lee was familiar with Tilly's day to day as she saw her at In Bloom several times a week and Tilly would tell her about classes and life. But she loved getting to hear about Michael and Ronin's business. The young men had opened a shared office space the prior summer and while it had some difficulties, they were pleased with their regular attendance and were dreaming about expansions.

Anna Lee pestered them with questions and was happy to hear Tilly share her own insights about her brother's and boyfriend's business. To an outsider, she may appear to be focused on fashion, beauty and having fun, but she had a business acumen about her. She gave Micheal and Ronin ideas about marketing and cost savings. All the more indication to Anna Lee that she would be successful no matter what she did. It was time to talk to her about taking over In Bloom.

Once they finished lunch, Anna Lee asked the men to unload bags of compost she'd bought the day before. Since she had to drive the van anyway, she made the best of it and stopped for garden supplies. They left to change and unload the car while Anna Lee and Tilly cleaned the kitchen.

"Tilly," Anna Lee began, "have you given any more thought to what you'll do after you graduate? Any job offers lined up?"

Tilly shrugged, her hands in the sink. Suds were as far up as her elbows. "I've sent my resume out, but nothing has come up yet. I want to stay here since Ronin is here. I don't think it would be beneficial to our relationship if I moved away for a job."

"Long distance is hard." She thought about the day that Gene left for the service. She'd known it was going to be hard, but she'd bought new stationery to stay in touch and they'd promised each other that they would ride the storm out and come out stronger for it. But fate had other plans. "I mentioned before that maybe you could consider taking over In Bloom. I would like you to really give that some serious thought."

"Right. You did. I've just been so focused on school and Ronin; I haven't given that serious thought yet. To be honest, though, I don't know that I could do it. It would be tough having all the responsibility on my shoulders. I don't think I can do it. Own my own business."

The sound of Ronin and Michael laughing outside caught both of their attention.

Anna Lee smiled. "Tilly, you provide your brother and Ronin helpful guidance when they talk about their business. You have the right instincts and skills. You'd be fabulous. I can spend more time training you on floral design, but the business management side, you've got that down pat."

Tilly rinsed a plate and put it in the drainer. "Maybe. But it seems like it would be hard to figure the legal stuff."

"I hear you. I couldn't do it either. But that's what lawyers and accountants are for. I'm due for a meeting with both soon. I'll start talking about what such a transition might look like. How much the business is worth and all that. I should talk to your mother, too. I need to think about estate planning and what that would mean to the estate."

"Right!" Tilly's eyes widened as she looked at Anna Lee. "I wouldn't want to take away from mom's inheritance. Not that you're going anywhere, anytime soon!"

"No, dear. I'm not. Unless the good lord has other plans for me." She laughed. "Don't worry about that. We'll make sure it's all up and up. For you, your mom and brother. If you're interested. It is a big commitment and maybe it's too much to put on your shoulders at your age. But I know you'd do well, and I'd love to see In Bloom pass on to the right person."

Anna Lee thought about how her genes had been passed to Tilly, though she hadn't had the benefit of watching Tilly grow into the amazing young woman she was today. Just looking at her, it was easy to see the family resemblance. Tilly's smile was so similar to her own, the way one corner pulled back when the smile got bigger.

Tilly got her dad's hazel eyes and his medium brown hair. Anna Lee enjoyed seeing that Irena had deep brown eyes, though it was impossible to know if they came from her or from Gene.

Their conversation was interrupted when the two young men came to the back door, sweating and dirty from lifting the heavy bags of soil and carrying them through the damp grass.

"Grandma," Michael said. "I'll come over this week and mow. It may be the last time this year. Don't you dare try to get the mower out yourself!"

Michael had mowed once already and found it crazy that Anna Lee had mowed the yard herself. Her lawn mower was ancient and didn't have the self-pulling capabilities newer models did.

"All right. I'll make you dinner if you do."

"Sounds like a plan. I'll let you know what night works best." He replied. "Tilly, we should get a move on. Ronin and I have to work on employee evaluations this afternoon."

"Yikes!" Tilly cried. "We've finished the cleanup so I can go. We'll get out of your hair, Grannie Annie." She turned to the woman and pulled her into a hug. "I'll think about what you said. I'm excited about the idea. If you've really got the faith in me."

"I do, dear. I do."

CHAPTER TWENTY-EIGHT

THE SUNDAY BEFORE Christmas, John drove Anna Lee to Chicago to celebrate the holiday with Irena and her family. Anna Lee was disappointed that she couldn't be with her daughter on the holiday itself–Irena's husband had booked them a family cruise months before they found out about Anna Lee–so John was determined to make Christmas extra special.

On Christmas Day, John drove to Anna Lee's to pick her up at six-thirty in the morning to take her to his house for the day. He wanted to be sure that they were back before his grandkids woke up.

His house was full, and it was a relief to sneak out and take a breath of air. Everyone had arrived two nights before, and Christmas Eve had been filled with games, movies, and baking.

Anna Lee had come over for Christmas Eve dinner and to watch "A Christmas Carol", the 1951 version with Alastair Sim, John's favorite. She had attended several family functions that summer and fall and was settling into his family life nicely.

John had decided it was time to ask her to marry him. Although he thought it might be a cop-out to give an engagement ring as a Christmas gift, that's what he was planning, but not in front of the family. He was sure of Anna Lee's affection for him and fairly certain she'd say yes, but it wasn't a moment to be shared with his family. He planned to propose in the evening, after he had taken her home.

Anna Lee's voice pulled him from his musings. "The light turned green five seconds ago, John. Hurry up! Those grandbabies are going to be awake and in the front of the tree, and we're going to miss the look of wonder on their faces if you don't get a move on."

"Yes, ma'am," he laughed. It was amazing to see that she was as excited as he was.

They pulled into the driveway, and Anna Lee flew out of the passenger seat almost before he turned off the engine.

She was carrying a large tote bag and a baking dish of cheesy potatoes that she'd made for Christmas dinner.

He met her in front of the car and offered to take something from her hands.

"Take the bag, please," she said, lifting her arm.

INSIDE THE HOUSE, they found Tara and Kelley in the kitchen. The smell of cinnamon rolls and coffee permeated the space.

"Morning, ladies," Anna Lee said, putting the pan on the counter.

"I'll take these to the living room," John said to her, indicating the tote bag. "Can I put them under the tree?"

"Don't know what else you'd do with them," she teased.

Tara popped up from her seat, walked up to Anna Lee, and pulled her into a tight hug. "Hi. I'm glad you're here."

Anna Lee closed her eyes and hugged the young woman back. She was thankful for how far their relationship had come. Tara often called Anna Lee or popped by her house to visit on her own. She said she felt at ease in Anna Lee's home, as if a weight lifted from her shoulders every time she walked in. Anna Lee thought that was the greatest compliment anyone could give her.

"I am, too," she finally said, releasing Tara. "Don't get up," she said to Kelley, walking over and giving her a hug. "The kiddos are still sleeping?"

"Yep. Hopefully, it'll be another hour before they're up. We let them stay up a little late last night. If they're up too early, I worry about breakdowns before noon."

"With Santa and presents? There can't be any breakdowns on Christmas," Anna Lee replied. "Smells delicious in here."

"Tara's making breakfast for us."

Anna Lee turned to Tara, who had pulled the oven door ajar. "Anything I can do to help?"

"No, I got it."

"I'm sure you do. I'll go check on John, then."

BACK AT HOME, after a glorious Christmas celebration with John's family, Anna Lee settled into her loveseat and pulled a throw blanket over her legs. John was in the kitchen getting them glasses of wine. After the long day, she didn't think she needed any more wine, but John insisted. Salty jumped up beside her and curled up to sleep after a few caresses.

"Here we are," John said, entering the room with two glasses in one hand and a bottle in the other. He set the bottle on the coffee table, handed a glass to Anna Lee, and sat in the chair next to her.

"Whoa, what a fantastic but exhausting day," Anna Lee said, taking a sip.

"It was with those kids around. I nearly wept with relief when Kelley put them down for a nap."

"I bet it wasn't easy getting them to nod off," Anna Lee said, setting her drink down and pulling the throw higher. "They were little balls of frenetic energy. All those gifts and the cookies. Thank you for the invite. I had a great day."

"It wouldn't have been the same without you. Everyone agreed."

"Did you take a poll?" Anna Lee teased.

"No need to." He shook his head. "I know them all well. I know you missed Irena and her family today, but I think the day was almost perfect," he continued, putting his glass down. "I have one more gift for you." He stood up and reached into his pocket.

Anna Lee watched with curiosity. He'd given her a beautiful Pandora silver charm bracelet earlier. He'd included every flower charm he could find—pink and purple tulips, pansies, roses, and daisies. It was precious! What was he doing now?

He knelt down in front of her, and Anna Lee started to cry. She'd seen this in movies. This is where he proposes! Gah! Her whole body vibrated with anticipation.

"Anna Lee Foster," he began. "I don't think I have the words to express how much you mean to me. And I don't want to come pick you up on special days. I want to wake up with you on those special days and every day. I promise I'll be the best husband that I can be. And I'll be a good cat-dad to Salty. Will you please say you'll marry me?"

Anna Lee blinked, swiping at her eyes. She couldn't believe this was happening. "Yes, John, I'll marry you."

He leaned forward to kiss her, and she threw her arms around him. Salty was not happy with all the commotion, so he jumped off the loveseat and meowed from the middle of the room.

After a few more kisses, John leaned back, showing her the ring. "You didn't even look at the ring."

She finally looked. It was an antique ring with a large opal stone surrounded by filigree details. She gasped. "John, it's gorgeous."

"I hoped you'd like it. It reminded me of you when I saw it. The pinks and purples in the stone reminded me of your favorite colors. And the dainty, swirling details reminded me of the Victorian home you love so much. If it's not to your liking, we can look for something else."

"No! This is perfect." She held out her hand, and he slid it onto her finger. "What do your girls say? Did they know you were doing this?"

"They did. They are all supportive, and they can't wait to talk to you. When you're ready."

"It'll be a big change for them. Nothing we must rush into."

"Right. We don't have to set a date. We can have a long engagement."

"Yes, there are things to do before we marry. Estate planning stuff. Maybe we should each retire before we marry, too."

"I love the sound of that. I'll be ready to put in my resignation in a few months. I want to hit that thirty-year anniversary first."

"Great goal. And I…" She paused and took in a breath. "I need to come up with a plan for In Bloom. It's such a huge piece of who I am and who I've been. I need to find the right owner to take it over. I hope another florist will take on the business."

"All right. Let's have a toast." They picked up their glasses. "To lots of big things in the year ahead. Retirement for me. Selling In Bloom for you. And maybe a wedding, to boot."

"Hear, hear!" She clinked his glass and took a sip.

December 25th–It's just before midnight and I should be exhausted as the day started early. I wanted to be at John's house before his grandbabies woke up. But I can't sleep! I'll probably be awake all night.

Once John brought me home, I thought we'd have a quick glass of wine to unwind, and he'd go home. Though he took a long nap this afternoon, I could tell he was tired. Those children are tiring and I'm not just talking about the babies. Haha!

I thought he wanted the drink to unwind but turns out he wanted it to toast—to our ENGAGEMENT!

He asked me to marry him in the front room. He got down on one knee and pulled a beautiful antique ring out of his pocket and asked. Of course, I said yes.

As soon as he left, I called Irena. I felt bad interrupting her family vacation, but I wanted to share. She shrieked with joy, and I could tell she was crying. It was the sweetest response. She said she would tell the rest of her family right away. Tilly called me ten minutes later, with Michael close by. They both congratulated me.

Weird. In the past, I would always call Tabitha with any news. This is the first time in many, many years that she wasn't the first call I made. I'll call her tomorrow.

I can't wait to marry John, though we aren't in a big rush. There are details to be worked out. Those details don't matter now. I'm just ecstatic to know that one day in the future, we will begin an amazing life together. I hope we have many, many years together. Many years of family celebrations, both his and mine—ours.

Thank you, Jesus, on your birthday, for giving me the greatest blessings imaginable.

CHAPTER TWENTY-NINE

SIX MONTHS LATER

ANNA LEE NOTICED her hand shaking as she applied her pale pink lipstick. "Come on, lady. This is one of the best days of your life. There's no need to be nervous," she told herself.

She heard John walking around downstairs and knew he was double checking that everything was in place.

She was certain everything was ready; she'd spent the last week cleaning the house and preparing for today. Nothing was out of place, and everything was ready to go. Still, she appreciated that John cared enough to take another look.

Standing slowly, she took a breath, looking at herself in the corner mirror. She had on a lavender-colored dress with pale pink rosebuds. Her gray hair was pulled back in a chignon, and a hair comb with pale pink rosebuds held it in place. She kept her jewelry simple: a pair of dangling light pink pearl earrings with a matching necklace.

"It'll have to do," she told her reflection.

She slipped on her slingback sandals and walked towards the door. Exiting the bedroom, she flipped off the light and took a quick glance back at the room. She smiled, thinking about John staying with her tonight for the first time.

Downstairs, she found John in the kitchen and admired him for a moment before he knew she was there. He was wearing charcoal gray slacks, a white button-down shirt, and a lavender tie that matched her dress perfectly. His suit jacket was lying on the back of the banquet seat near the window.

"I think I'm ready," she said.

He turned to her and sucked in a breath. "You look beautiful. It's not bad luck to see the bride before the wedding, is it?"

She gave a little shrug. "Since the wedding is a surprise to everyone else, we don't have a choice. And I never believed in that old superstition, anyway. Taking flowers to brides for over forty years, I've seen many who've met with their groom before the ceremony, and I never heard of it causing bad luck."

John stepped closer and pulled her into an embrace, giving her a quick kiss on the cheek. "Do you think we have everyone fooled?"

"No one has seemed suspicious to me."

She had sent an invitation to a "Semi-Formal Spring Garden Party" to their closest family and friends. They were expecting around twenty-five guests. The invitation asked the ladies to wear something floral and the men to wear slacks and spring colors. Since everyone knew how much she loved to tend to her flower beds, all the more now that she was retired, she hoped it seemed likely enough.

Anna Lee had been ecstatic when she'd approached Tilly about buying In Bloom. It had been apparent that Tilly was going to remain in Bloomington, as her relationship with her boyfriend, Ronin, flourished. It didn't take much convincing for Tilly to seize the opportunity to take over the shop. Anna Lee worked hard to make the transition as seamless as possible. Once that was complete, she'd jumped into retirement life with both feet.

They expected everyone to arrive by one. The invitation had promised finger foods and hors d'oeuvres, which the guests would partake of as they gathered around the house and yard. Then, around two, the officiant—who they would introduce as Anna Lee's new neighbor—would get everyone's attention and gather them together for the ceremony.

John laughed and squeezed her a little tighter. "Feels like we're trying to pull off a heist."

"A heist of their hearts, maybe."

Salty rubbed against and wound through their legs. John looked down.

"Do you have a lint roller?" he asked.

Anna Lee laughed. "That durn cat. Here." She opened a cabinet and pulled out a small roller. "This'll do."

There was a knock on the back door, and someone yelled, "Yoo hoo!"

Anna Lee went to the door to find the two catering assistants who would serve appetizers and drinks to the guests. "Hello. Let me show you where everything is. Guests should arrive soon."

THEY'D RENTED SEVERAL tall wicker tables and scattered throughout the backyard to hold drinks and plates. On top of each table was either a floral vase or a floral tea kettle filled with blooms. Some arrangements had soft pink peonies, others contained tulips, and still others white calla lilies. Anna Lee loved the variety and was happy she still had the contact information for the best suppliers. She couldn't have worked with Tilly at In Bloom on the flowers, or the surprise would have been ruined.

They were in the backyard, where Anna Lee was showing John some peonies beginning to bloom, when the guests started to arrive.

John's daughter Tara and her boyfriend Luke were the first, followed closely by Anna Lee's cousin Tabitha and her son Sam. Tabitha's other son, Vic, was out of town and unable to attend.

The rest of the guests arrived, and soon the backyard was filled with everyone they loved and cherished, including many former employees of Anna Lee's at In Bloom—Paige with her husband Trevor, Lauren with her fiancé Hawk, and Nica and her long-term boyfriend Grady.

Then there were their family members: John's daughter Kelley and her family, his other daughter Deana and her husband, Anna Lee's newly found daughter Irena and her family, Tilly and Ronin, and Michael and his new girlfriend Shevaun.

Anna Lee was pleased that everyone had taken the invitation's instructions to heart and dressed for the occasion. She handed out compliments on clothing and hairstyles like candy on Halloween.

Only two people seemed a little suspicious: her cousin Tabitha and Tilly. They pulled Anna Lee aside and asked, "What's going on?" Anna Lee simply said, "I wanted to show off the gorgeous yard—look at all the flowers blooming!" and led them around to look at the flowers.

Vince, the "neighbor", gave Anna Lee a significant glance, and she pulled Tabitha aside, asking for her help in the kitchen for a moment.

In the kitchen, Tabitha asked where the cat was, and Anna Lee said he was probably in hiding because of all the people trampling in and out. Then she opened a box on the counter and pulled out a small bouquet of three white roses, elegant greenery, and a pale lavender ribbon.

She turned to her cousin. "Tabby, I'm getting married. Will you be my lady of honor?" Anna Lee couldn't bring herself to call her sixty-seven-year-old widowed cousin either a maid or a matron.

"What?!" Tabitha shrieked. "I knew something was up! You have got to be kidding!"

"Not kidding. John and I are getting hitched."

Tabitha pressed her hands to her mouth, and tears sprang to her eyes.

"Don't you start crying, Tabby! You'll make me cry, and this is a joyous occasion." Anna Lee wagged her finger in Tabitha's direction.

A caterer stepped into the kitchen. "Anna Lee, if you're ready, we'll get the champagne bottles out."

"I'm ready. We should be ready for champagne in ten minutes." She turned back to Tabitha. "Can you pull yourself together? Here's a tissue." She reached into the box on the counter and handed one to her cousin.

"Oh, mercy! I can't believe this is happening. What do I do?" Tabitha asked, dabbing at her cheeks.

"Just hold this bouquet and walk out the back door. As soon as he sees you, the officiant will get everyone's attention. You walk toward him. It's Vince, the guy in the purple shirt. He'll be standing by John. You walk out to them and stand on the left side. I'll follow behind you. Then the ceremony will begin. We'll be done in ten minutes, tops. Got it?"

"No rehearsal…" Tabitha muttered.

"No lots of things, but this is what we want. Everyone we love is here. Well, except Vic. Couldn't be helped."

"Wow! This is wild!" Tabitha took the bouquet, and Anna Lee picked up her own bouquet, as well as the boutonnière that she would clip on John's lapel.

Anna Lee followed closely behind Tabitha, peeking around her cousin. As planned, once Tabitha stood in the doorway for a moment, "neighbor" officiant Vince gave a loud whistle.

"Can I have your attention, everyone?" he said, when everyone paused at the earsplitting noise. "You thought you were invited to a plain old garden party. But is there truly such a thing? Plain.

Old. Garden Party, I mean." Everyone laughed. "Well, that was just half the story."

John stepped up to the officiant and Anna Lee could hear several gasps as people caught on.

Vince chuckled. "As a few of you may have guessed, John and Anna Lee have decided to make their devotion to each other official, and they are going to tie the knot with all of us here as witnesses."

"What?"

"No!"

"Are you kidding?"

Shouts and exclamations of glee could be heard from all corners of the yard.

Vince continued. "If you could all gather closer." People moved in. "Please leave a path from here to the back door," he said, gesturing. "We'll begin."

Tabitha turned back to Anna Lee. "No music?"

"The birds are singing. That's music enough for me."

"Aw," Tabitha said, more tears slipping down her face. She dabbed again, turned around, and began walking down the stairs.

THE LOOKS OF surprise and pure joy on everyone's faces made Anna Lee even more excited about the afternoon. She could not wait to marry John and felt thrilled that their families were there to witness the occasion.

She didn't have the same expectations about marriage as a twenty-something would. There would be no babies for her and John, nor the joy of watching little ones of their own grow up. There wouldn't be the expectation of decades together. That was a possibility, but not an expectation at their ages.

But none of that dampened her joy. Whether she and John had ten years together or ten months, it would be blissful; she was sure of it. They were meant to be together for this time in their lives.

And while they wouldn't have those children of their own, she fully expected to have several grandbabies and great-grandbabies, between John's daughters and her own newly found grandchildren, Tilly and Michael.

Unbeknownst to Anna Lee, Salty had dashed out the door with her and was now ambling towards John, sort of like a flower cat. She wished she'd put a floral collar around him.

Her eyes bounced between John and their guests. She laughed when she saw John grab the man nearest to him, Alex, Kelley's husband, to be his best man. She smiled, seeing some of her family members on the "groom's side" and some of his family on the "bride's side". They had been standing around, talking in little clusters, when Vince had called them to attention. They were so shocked, no one thought or cared about dividing up across the aisle of freshly mowed grass.

Her daughter, Irena, was standing near the officiant, beaming. Anna Lee reached over and clasped her hand as she approached. Irena squeezed her hand and leaned over and kissed her cheek. Anna Lee blinked rapidly to stop the tears that threatened.

When she finally reached John, she slid the boutonnière onto his lapel. He grasped her hand and kissed her palm before they both turned towards the officiant. There was an audible sigh from the guests at his gesture.

"Beloved family and friends," Vince began, "while it seems to have come as a shock to all of you…" The crowd laughed, "…we are here to witness the marriage of John and Anna Lee. They told you I was just a neighbor, but that's not true…"

Anna Lee half-listened to Vince's words. She was thinking about everything that had happened in her life to lead her here to this moment. Taking a deep breath, she thought about her parents. She had forgiven them long ago for their inability to accept the child she delivered and gave up for adoption. They weren't perfect people, and times were different then. A memory of dancing around their living room, standing on her daddy's feet when she was three or four years old, hit her like a tidal wave, and she nearly gasped aloud. She tightened her shoulders to stave off the threat of sobs that seized her. She remembered the laughter, and she wished for a moment that he could have been here walking her down the aisle, though he would have been nearly one hundred years old if he were still alive.

John tilted his head, a question in his eyes. She lifted a corner of her mouth to let him know she was fine.

After the ceremony and the announcement of "Mr. and Mrs. Peerson", John and Anna Lee turned to face their guests. John lifted his hand in the air, raising Anna Lee's with it. "Ta da!" he yelled joyfully.

Irena, Tilly, and Tara rushed forward, throwing their arms around each other as they shared ecstatic hugs with the newlyweds.

"Oh, Grannie Annie!" Tilly exclaimed as she gave Anna Lee a bear hug. "That was the most amazingly scrumptious wedding I've ever attended! I'm just busting with happiness for you!"

Anna Lee embraced her granddaughter. "I can't imagine being any happier than I am now. Until your wedding, darlin'."

Tilly laughed. "We'll see. Now, about this new family. John's daughters are now Mom's stepsisters and my…" She paused and pursed her lips with a comical tilt to her head. "Step-aunts! What a riot! Aunt Tara!" she exclaimed. "Aunt Kelley! Get over here!"

Anna Lee laughed and shook her head. That girl.

CHAPTER THIRTY

EPILOGUE

ANNA LEE WALKED into the front room carrying a tray with four cups of hot chocolate, a bottle of Bailey's Irish Cream, a bowl of mini marshmallows, and several peppermint candy canes. It was the Sunday after Thanksgiving, and Tilly, Deana, and Tara were helping Anna Lee and John put up and decorate the Christmas tree. John had insisted on buying an eight-foot-tall fresh fir tree. He wasn't as content as Anna Lee was with the silver artificial tree she'd had for over thirty years. He didn't trust that its electrical cord wouldn't burst into flames. Besides, he'd done the research and showed Anna Lee how the tree farm where he got the tree used a rental model; after Christmas, they would come and get the tree and replant it on their farm. They would do this for several years until the tree outgrew the ability to be reused and would retire to a lovely grove on the farm—an environmentally friendly alternative to a single-use tree.

She didn't like admitting to John that she adored the smell of the live fir in the house. Whenever she caught the scent, it made her smile.

Setting the tray on the coffee table, she assessed the progress being made. John had strung all the lights, and the girls were sorting through her extensive collection of ornaments. They had ooh-ed and ah-ed over the collection as they unpacked them. Anna Lee had countless handblown glass ornaments in pale pastel colors covered in glitter. John groaned about the glitter but smiled as he did it.

"Anna Lee," Tara said, lifting a small glass bluebird ornament. "These birds are beautiful. I love that you have so many little birds."

"Birds belong in the trees. Especially Christmas trees. Take a break and get some cocoa while it's still hot."

"Yummy!" Tilly said, placing an ornament with other pink ones.

"Sounds good," Tara agreed.

They each grabbed a cup and took a seat as John settled in his recliner. Anna Lee looked at him and smiled. He seemed comfortable and natural here, as though he'd been here for eight years, not eight months.

"How are things going at the shop, Tilly?" Anna Lee asked. "Ready for the Christmas rush?"

"I think so. I'm a little worried about Mackenzie, though. She seems to be unusually stressed about the latest play she's in. She got the lead role, and she says it's taking an emotional toll on her. Honestly, I think it has more to do with her gorgeous co-lead than the role itself."

"You don't say. Go on."

"Well." Tilly tilted her head as she considered her words. "She won't say for certain, but I think she has a crush on him, and it seems to add pressure to perform well."

"Sounds tough," Tara chimed in. "When is the play? I'd love to see your roommate act."

"In early February. I'll send you the information on tickets. Maybe we could all get a block of tickets together."

"I'd love to go. What about you, John?" Anna Lee asked her husband.

"Sounds great!" John leaned forward and added another spoonful of marshmallows to his cocoa. "Mack is a smart kid. I'm sure she'll figure things out."

"I hope so," Tilly said, looking doubtful. "She's lost weight and says she's not sleeping well. I've never seen her stressed like this."

"Why don't you bring her by next week for a visit? I'll bake something yummy and try to fatten her up." Anna Lee smiled to make light of the comments, but if Tilly was worried about her friend, Anna Lee was worried, too.

"Tara, how's work going, hon?" she asked.

"Great! I finally got the promotion that I wanted, and—drum roll please!" She paused dramatically, and Tilly drummed on the coffee table. "I'm taking my first trip to Milan for a home interior show in March!"

Tilly shrieked, "Awesome!" At the same time, Anna Lee said, "Wonderful!"

John chuckled. "I always said you are going places, kiddo."

"Thank you," Tara said, looking at each of them, her blonde hair swishing across her shoulders.

Anna Lee admired the young woman. She knew what she wanted, and she went for it. She never let doubt or fear hold her back. Admirable traits.

Stirring her hot chocolate with the candy cane, Anna Lee leaned back on the couch and patted Tara's leg. Thinking over the last couple of years, Anna Lee was still amazed at how things had turned out. Instead of facing the rest of her life alone, afraid to retire, she now faced the future boldly with a great man by her side and a lovely, melded family. Between her and John, they now had four kids, four grandkids…and perhaps a few more on the way!

WHAT'S NEXT

Thank you for reading Wildflowers for Anna Lee. Your honest review will help future readers decide if they want to take a chance on a new-to-them author. Please consider leaving an honest review on Amazon or Goodreads or wherever you normally leave reviews.

There is a bonus scene available when you join my newsletter. Visit this link to download a copy–https://BookHip.com/RNTVTAJ

I hope you're rooting for all the In Bloom ladies. Anna Lee's employees are an amazing group of young women and have a lot of stories to tell.

Here's a look at the other books in this series.

Paige is a bookworm with big plans. Trevor is a flirty handyman searching for joy. Can they find common ground and plant a lifelong passion? If you like opposites who attract, lighthearted humor, and wise older characters, then you'll enjoy Peonies for Paige! https://www.amazon.com/dp/B0B8GD3H1K

Nica's a quiet, free spirit. Grady is bossy and by the book. Will a rough renovation help them discover the charms of true love? If you like multicultural characters, workplace chemistry, and stories that tackle modern issues, then you'll adore Dahlias for Dominica! https://www.amazon.com/dp/B0B9T6GN61

Lauren has set her sights on the big city. Hawk adores the untouched wilderness. Are they hiking toward heartbreak or happily ever after? If you like unexpected pairings, nurturing male characters, and upbeat adventures, then you'll love Lilies for Lauren! https://www.amazon.com/gp/product/B0BLWF251T

Tilly's trying to get it all together. Ronin's been crushing on her for years. Will a swoon-worthy first kiss plant the seed for happily ever after? If you like impulsive heroines, workplace families, and watching friends fall head over heels, then you'll love the search for belonging in Tulips for Tilly! https://www.amazon.com/gp/product/B0BTMVP1PM

All of these books are in Kindle Unlimited. Paperback and Hardback copies are also available on Amazon, Barnes & Noble, and Bookshop.org.

ACKNOWLEDGEMENTS

First, I want to thank my husband, Tim, for supporting my writing dream. Thank you for being my sounding board, my inspiration, and my champion. I don't know what I would do without you. I love you!

A huge shout out to Paulette W for beta reading—thank you for your comments and attention to detail!

Family is everything, and I owe a sincere thank you to my siblings, siblings-in-law, aunts, uncles, cousins, nieces, and nephews for all the encouragement. I love you infinitely.

Thank you to the professionals that supported this project—Marisa F for Development Editing, Rebecca H for copy editing, Stacy U for proofreading, and Stephanie and Melissa at Alt 19 Creative for the gorgeous book cover and interior formatting!

And a heartfelt thank you to you, dear reader, for taking a chance on this story.

ABOUT THE AUTHOR

Kasey Kennedy is an Illinois gal through and through. She grew up in Central Illinois, finished college at Southern Illinois University Carbondale, and, soon afterwards, moved to Chicago. She's been in Chicago or the surrounding suburbs ever since.

Kasey is happily married to her husband Tim and loves nothing more than spending time with him—especially when that involves live music! If not attending a live show, they are usually enjoying evenings on the deck, listening to music, visiting their large families, watching movies, or planning their next trip.

When not dreaming up new characters and new stories, Kasey is reading or planning what to read next. Occasionally, she pulls out the guitar that she has been trying to learn for 30+ years and strums enough to annoy her cat, Pepper.

FACEBOOK:

https://www.facebook.com/kaseykennedy8/

INSTAGRAM:

https://www.instagram.com/kaseykennedy8/

WEBSITE:

https://www.kasey-kennedy.com